THE PROMISE

ELLA SAGE

For my wonderful husband and family

Prologue

LACEY- 10 YEARS AGO

"Are you scared? You know, enlisting in the marines?" I asked Gage, tightening my grip on his hand as we strolled around Lake Johnson. Gage stopped in his tracks and turned to face me, his dark eyes locking with mine.

"What do you think?" He sighed, then he pulled me into his chest and kissed the top of my head. "I'm not scared of being a marine. Losing you forever is my deepest fear."

His thin frame trembled against mine, and I felt his heart beating against my ear as our hug deepened.

Gage had been my first at just about everything. For the last two years of high school we'd been inseparable, unable to be apart for any stretch of time. The tall, thin and handsome eighteen-year-old had stolen my heart at the beginning of our junior year, and the night we graduated we'd skipped the parties and headed to his family's beach house on the outer banks. There we shared our true feelings for the first time, both with words and our bodies.

"I love you so much, Lacey." Gage's deep voice trembled,

and his grip on me grew stronger. "How am I going to survive without you?"

A tear slid down my cheek, because the same fear filled me with an ache I'd never experienced before. I felt Gage's fingers on the back of my neck, and seconds later, he was staring into my eyes again.

"Let's run away."

The pressure behind my eyes burned, because I wanted nothing more than to be by his side. His thumb swiped at the tears now flowing freely down my cheeks. Gage's full lips inched closer to my mouth, and seconds later they crashed against mine, taking my breath away. I could feel his excitement pressing against my stomach, and heat surged through me. My girlfriends had all complained about having sex with their boyfriends, how all the hype around their first time had only led to disappointment and guilt.

Making love to Gage was different. We'd both been each other's first, and the emotional and physical bond between us had only deepened with every encounter.

There had been many sleepless nights where I lay awake, wondering what it would be like to marry Gage, and to wake up in his arms every morning.

"Please," I moaned, breaking the kiss, "you know I want to be with you, more than anything else in the world."

"Then let's do it. Between our savings and graduation gifts we can afford to strike out on our own." Gage's voice cracked. I placed my hands against his chest and gently pushed him away.

"We can't do that." I sniffed, and backed out of his arms and paced, hugging myself. "Not that I don't want to, but…"

"You can still go to college." Gage interrupted. "We couldn't afford Harvard medical school, but we…"

"I have to go. As much as I care for you, Gage, being a surgeon has been my lifelong dream, and graduating from Harvard would open up almost any door for me." Without thinking, I placed a lock of my strawberry-blonde hair in my mouth, a habit I'd broken in middle school.

Gage abruptly turned away and stalked a few feet ahead. That was when I noticed his shoulders shaking, and my resolve threatened to break. As much as I wanted to be a doctor, how could I let go of this love so soon? I sighed, then picked up a stone from the path and skimmed it across the water.

"Damn it," I whispered. "Why do we have to choose?"

"I'm sorry," Gage murmured. "I shouldn't be pressuring you like this. You're going to be in Florida for the rest of the summer, and I'm heading to Parris Island for basic training in three days. You have your whole life ahead of you, and so do I." He sighed, then wrapped his arm around my waist and we both stared across the lake.

I could hear honking in the distance, and moments later a flock of Canada Geese descended. They'd always frightened me, especially when they defended their nests. But that fear didn't even come close to the terror I felt now at losing Gage.

"Does it really have to end?" I murmured, knowing the answer before I asked.

"I don't want it to, Lacey. But I have to serve four years in the marines, and then Dad wants me to join his firm. Shit." He muttered, stepping away and kicking a stone into the water, provoking a flutter of wings from the geese now swimming a few feet away.

"I'll be in med school. Never-ending school." I sighed, both dreading my new life and excited to start it. "We can't…

we just can't make it, not with all these obstacles in front of us."

I strolled over to where Gage stood, and placed my hands on his chest. "You are my first love, Gage, and no one will ever take that away from me."

His brown eyes were wet, and he glanced up to the darkening sky, and gulped. "Let's make a promise."

I raised an eyebrow and nodded for him to continue.

"Both of us have a bunch of things happening over the next few years, so yeah, a long-distance relationship isn't going to…" Gage turned his head and swiped at his eyes, then met my gaze again. "In ten years' time, if we both are still single, let's meet at our high school reunion and maybe we can…"

"Pick up from where we're leaving it now?" I whispered, a flicker of hope radiating throughout my chest. Then, it dawned on me that the likelihood of that happening was close to zero.

Gage nodded, his face softening while his cheeks burned red. It felt like someone had punched me in the stomach, and I'd do anything in the world to see his teeth split into a smile.

"I promise you, Gage, in ten years we will be together, though I don't know how I'm going to wait so long."

"This isn't over, Lacey, and it never will be. I promise you will always have my heart, and if I have to wait until…"

"Stop." I reached up and laid a finger across his lips. "I can't bear this anymore." A sob threatened, and I didn't want to make our goodbye more painful than it was.

"I love you, Lacey." Gage kissed the tip of my finger, then brushed his lips across mine.

"I love you too, Gage." I whispered, then we both turned

toward the lake and watched the water turn orange from the setting sun. “Don’t you ever forget that.”

Chapter One

LACEY

"Are you excited to meet your new colleagues?" The woman from human resources asked in the cramped and nearly airless elevator. Her demeanor was cool and professional. It was packed, the doors opening on every floor, letting people in and out. A gurney took up half the space, forcing the two of us against the rear wall.

I knew I should answer quickly, laced with my best sincere smile. But the ball of anxiety spinning in my gut made that difficult to do. It was my first day of work at the UNC Rex Hospital in the ER. I'd moved home to Raleigh from Boston to make a fresh start in my hometown. It was comforting to see familiar places, but starting a new job was stressful, especially after being gone for so long. Ten years in Boston, the last four spent nursing at Tufts Medical Center. Finally, my lips stretched across my face in a semblance of a smile, and I managed a small nod.

"Well, the staff are looking forward to meeting you, and they will put you to work right away. The emergency room is always hopping. Never a dull moment." A phone vibrated in her pocket. She pulled it out, raised an eyebrow, and scowled.

"I thought I'd have time to show you around the floor, but an emergency of my own has come up." She said, and I must have made a face. "Don't worry, I won't leave you stranded. I have someone who will work with you for the next two weeks to make sure you learn the correct procedures." Her eyes never connected with mine, and the ball of anxiety bounced up to my rib cage.

Human resources was on the fourteenth floor, so by the time the elevator doors slid open on the first, I was ready to race out of the cramped space. I'd never been claustrophobic before, but my nerves were on edge. It felt like day one of school again, not knowing anyone or anything. I glanced at the woman's name tag. Zenovia. I knew the woman meant well, but her stiff demeanor left something to be desired. Oh, and her perfume was a powdery rose that overwhelmed the small space we were in.

It took every ounce of self-control not to run out of the elevator and straight through the sliding doors on the other side of the ER. I waited for Zenovia to exit first, and when I stepped on to the floor I was amazed at the calm. This was a gigantic hospital, and I expected it to be a madhouse from the get go. Instead, the staff patiently went about their business. A few of them were standing together, obviously gossiping, but when they saw Zenovia, they parted in a hurry. Apparently, she was someone they didn't want to cross.

"Lacey?" Zenovia's grin was gone, and she was glaring at her watch.

"I'm sorry, what were you saying?" My cheeks burned, caught not paying attention.

"That's okay, but I need to be on the ninth floor immediately. Come with me." She hurried toward the nurses' station in the middle of the ward.

"Nancy, where's Powell?" She asked a nurse, an older woman with a neutral smile she assumed as soon as she noticed Zenovia heading her way.

"Powell's at the pharmacy, but he should be back any minute. Would you like me to page him?" She said, picking up the phone.

"No, that won't be necessary. Nancy, this is Lacey Barnes. She's moved here from Boston and today is her first day on staff. I have to leave Lacey here with you. Something has come up, or I'd stay with her myself. Powell is expecting her, so let him know Lacey is here as soon as he returns to the floor." She turned without another word and jogged toward the elevator. Nancy's mouth opened to reply, but Zenovia was already gone. Her eyebrow lifted, and she shook her head.

"It's a pleasure to meet you. They scheduled me for my break five minutes ago. If you don't mind I'm going to let you sit in an empty office until Powell returns." She reached under the counter and pulled out a thick binder, and handed it to me. It was a manual of procedures, and must have weighed ten pounds. "This way." She led me down the hall and deposited me in a small gray room with a single window.

"I'm sorry, but you've arrived when it's relatively calm. I need to take my break now, otherwise, well, you know what it's like." She shook her head, then shut the door behind her.

I sat at a plain metal desk. There were no pictures or decorations, only the familiar smell of disinfectant. I opened the manual, prepared to at least give it a cursory glance, but my thoughts wandered to why I was here in the first place.

"You've come full circle, home again." I whispered, then turned in the chair and looked out the window. A mixture of students and staff were walking up and down the sidewalk. A few in pairs, but most had their heads down, hurrying to their destinations. Since I was new, I had few responsibilities, and I envied them their sense of purpose. The most pressing thing on my to-do list was finding a reputable hairdresser, who hopefully could wax my legs, too. My strawberry-blonde hair was so thick, I had to have it thinned out every few months, or it grew into a towering mess of split ends.

I'd arrived in Raleigh less than a week ago, escaping the chill of another Boston winter, or that's what I told myself. I'd spent ten years up north, only coming home for sporadic visits to my Aunt Millie. She'd graciously taken me in until I could find my own apartment. My parents had moved to Florida years ago, so she was my only family here. Since I hadn't maintained contact with anyone else in Raleigh, it felt like a fresh start.

I heard a thump outside the door and my knee jumped and hit the bottom of the desk. I flipped through the manual, keeping one eye on the door, hoping I appeared to be busy studying. Footsteps hurried away, and I sighed with relief, glad I wasn't caught daydreaming.

"No more doctors or men for that matter. You are to come to the hospital and leave alone." I spoke aloud, a faint echo filling the empty space.

I drummed my pink fingernails on the desk, impatient for this Powell person to put me to work. The longer I was alone, the more I could think of my humiliation. A few months ago I'd been jilted at the altar by Dr. Joseph Winthrop, abandoned for a younger surgical intern. It was for the best, since oddly enough, I hadn't missed him. On paper, he'd torn my heart to shreds. But what I didn't tell anyone, was that instead of pain, I felt relief. Like missing an airplane at the last minute and discovering it had crashed into the ocean later that day.

I thought I'd been in love with Joseph. He was supremely confident, and cocky, a top doctor in a crowded city teeming with ambitious doctors. In the rearview mirror though, he left me empty, devoid of passion. I'd only known true love once, but that was like a teenage dream, one you would wake up from, and despite closing your eyes over and over again, it's lost forever.

I'd loved my job, and despite the chilly winter, Boston was an amazing place to live. What drove me away were the gossips. They were thrilled to whisper about it all over Tufts Medical. It was humiliating, and Joseph only gave me a brief apology, never minding the trauma he had put me through. The pediatric ward I truly loved went from being the perfect work environment to a nightmare overnight. After a month of sideways glances and whispered speculation, I turned in my notice.

"You just had to shit where you eat, didn't you?" I reminded myself for the umpteenth time. This job would be different. Come to work, do my job, then go home. My heart was permanently encased in surgical steel, and if I had anything to say about it, it would stay that way.

The door burst open, and a man in scrubs stepped in, hands on hips and a broad smile plastered on his face.

"Hi! I'm Powell. You must be Lacey. Welcome to insanity." His hands spoke as loudly as his words. He had flaming red hair and freckles sprinkled across his nose. Powell's enthusiasm was infectious, and I returned his grin with a genuine one of my own.

"Nice to meet you, Powell." I started to stand, but he gestured for me to stay where I was.

"Sit, sit. It's quiet on the floor, which scares me. Whenever we get a lull, something insane happens." He sat across from me on the other side of the desk. "I was informed by her highness, Zenovia, that I am to be your mentor for the next two weeks. She's someone to be avoided at all costs, if you know what's best for you." He winked.

"Well, she does have a certain, um…" I started, then he burst into laughter.

"Oh my gawd, that look on your face is priceless. You are definitely going to fit in. Yes, a stick resides deep in her ass. Oh, and don't ever get trapped in an elevator with her. That godawful perfume would gag a maggot." He slapped his thigh and giggled, and moments later I giggled, too. Looked like my new job wouldn't be as boring as I thought. Boston was a crazy city, so I thought Raleigh would be a snore fest.

"Before I show you around, tell me a little about yourself. You'd better do it now, because at the drop of a hat this place can turn into a madhouse. Where did you work last?" Powell's bright blue eyes twinkled.

"I moved here from Boston. Worked at Tufts, in pediatrics." My gut clenched again, but this time it was a pang of regret. Had I made the right choice moving to Raleigh? There were other hospitals in Boston where I could've moved on with my life without coworkers knowing about my humiliation.

"Strange, you don't have an accent. I love Boston, oh and the beaches were beautiful, but I had the hardest time understanding anyone." Powell opened the office door and peeked out, checking to see if the floor was doing okay. When he closed it, I answered.

"I'm actually from Raleigh, moved away ten years ago. I guess that explains the lack of an accent. And yes, I used to go to the beach..." my mouth snapped shut while thoughts of long weekends with Joseph at his condo on Cape Cod flooded my mind. Status and luxury were my rewards for being with my ex, and though I missed that part, I certainly didn't miss him. Until I got to know Powell better, I'd keep my history to myself.

"Ah, sounds like a woman with a past. Tell me later over a cocktail. So, you come from pediatrics. Have you worked in ER before?" Powell asked, eyebrows coming together. He was probably nervous about training a total newbie.

"Yes, I worked in the ER for a couple of years, then I transferred to pediatrics for a change of pace. It can get pretty crazy there too." I said, then the door swung open. A young nurse with wide eyes interrupted us.

"Powell, there's been a multi-car pileup on New Bern Avenue. Get out here, the first ambulance is pulling up now." Adrenaline surged through my limbs and we both got to our feet. Powell held out his arm for me to go first.

"Welcome to the ER."

I leaned against the nurses' station and dabbed my brow with a tissue. Despite the chaos I felt fantastic. Work was exactly what I wanted, keeping my hands busy and my mind on anything but myself. Now that things had calmed down a little, they had me behind the desk until I knew more about how the department operated. At least, until the next big emergency.

"I brought you some lunch. Hope you like egg salad sandwiches. Let's go back to that office. Normally we'd eat in the cafeteria, but I want to make sure we're close by in case anything comes up." Powell grinned and walked away. I followed behind, trying to keep up with his quick steps. Damn, if it was like this everyday, I wouldn't have time to miss the slower pace of pediatrics.

"So how are you holding up?" He asked as I opened the white paper bag. I pulled out a soggy sandwich and was overwhelmed by hunger since I'd been too nervous about the new job to eat breakfast this morning.

"That was something else. I haven't been this busy in years." I mumbled, then scarfed down a quarter of the sandwich in one bite.

"You're going to be just fine. I can tell you've done this before. You were a big help, trust me. And hey, we've only got six more hours to go!" Powell laughed, then started on his own meal. A couple of minutes later he put down his food and spoke.

"For the rest of the shift you'll be working triage. I know you still don't know all the procedures, but it will help you learn the department better than anything else. Just check people in, and figure out the top priority cases. If you have any questions, page me. I'm sorry to eat and run, but I want to make sure Dr. Nash has everything he needs." Powell winked, his sly grin giving his game away.

"Which one was Dr. Nash?" I asked innocently, knowing exactly who the hot doctor was. I might be off of men, but he was a looker I'd immediately noticed as we took care of patients together. Blood rushed to Powell's face.

"Only the most delicious doctor in the hospital. Of course, he doesn't even know I'm alive. But I can dream." Powell sighed, then threw the remnants of his lunch in the trash. I bit my tongue, wanting to warn him away from nurse/doctor relationships. Joseph's face flashed in my mind, then I thought once again how my life would be so much better if I'd never pursued him.

"What's wrong? You look like you've seen a ghost." Powell asked, then stood. No way I'd let him in on my office romance humiliation. I needed to be professional, even if he wasn't.

"First day jitters I guess."

"My son thinks I'm having a heart attack."

"Let's see what is going on, Mr..." I asked, wanting to hear him say his name to figure out how alert he still was. When I saw the chart, warning bells went off inside my head. He was older, late fifties I guessed. The man looked familiar, and his commanding voice made me regret eating that awful sandwich for lunch.

"Patterson. Frank Patterson. My son and I were inspecting a property we might buy, and I felt a sharp pain in my chest. I think it's indigestion. Can't stand doctors, but Gage insisted he bring me in." The man had a domineering attitude that I was starting to remember from years ago. More importantly, I recognized his name.

"Dr. Nash will examine you, but before that you're getting an EKG." I said, then an older male nurse rolled the machine in.

"Perfect timing." I murmured, then I handed him the chart and beat a hasty retreat. Not only was the old man having a heart problem, but my own was suddenly pounding. The urge to hide in that gray, empty office overwhelmed me, but I hurried to the nurses' station instead.

As I circled the corner, I saw a tall, muscular man

standing at the nurses' station with his back to me. His dark brown hair was clipped short, and even though his hands were talking as loud as he was, through his panic he sounded like a man comfortable giving orders. He was speaking to a flustered nurse who was trying to calm him down.

"Is he okay? Dad's always been like Ironman. What's happening? Shit, I need to call Mom." The man reached into his back pocket for his phone.

"Damn it." I muttered. That deep baritone was so familiar, because it was the voice in my teenage dreams that haunted me to this day.

I caught a glimpse of the man's face, and in an instant his chestnut eyes locked with mine. The man had dark, rugged masculine looks that suggested arrogance, someone used to getting his own way. He cocked his head, then his eyebrows drew together. Without a second thought I turned on my heels and jogged around the corner, then leaned against the wall, breathless.

"It can't be him. My first day back and it's fucking Gage." I whispered, shaking my head. No way he would be here on the first day of my new job. Those sparkling brown eyes and sharp cheekbones were ingrained in my mind, never to be forgotten. And damn, he was built.

Father Time had been good to my ex-boyfriend. Gone was the skinny teenage boy I once loved. His pecs bulged under his tight red shirt, and I felt a flush spreading across my chest. Gage was standing only a few feet away, and instead of being elated, I wanted a hole in the ground to open up and swallow me.

I wrapped my arms around my chest and struggled to control my breathing. If this could have happened a few months from now, the timing would be perfect, but not on my first day of work. And especially not so soon after my last disastrous attempt at a relationship. An orderly pushing a patient in a wheelchair gave me an odd look as she passed.

"He probably doesn't remember you, or he has a girlfriend. Nobody that good looking is single, plus, you are not searching for a relationship. Pull yourself together, Lacey. This is your first day of work, so don't mess it up." I muttered, then straightened my back and strolled toward the nurses' station.

Gage was pacing in front of the desk, his phone pressed against his ear. I walked behind the counter and was about to hide in a supply closet when I heard my name called.

"Lacey?" Gage's deep voice rang out over the low roar of the ER. The skin on my arms pebbled at the sound, and my heart leapt into my throat. Damn it, I couldn't have a panic attack on the first day of work. I guessed there was no escaping the inevitable. Turning around, I tentatively gazed into those eyes that occasionally haunted my thoughts to this day. But they were fantasies, not reality. There was no way he could be the same boy I once loved after all these years.

"May I help you?" I replied, my voice scarcely above a whisper.

"It's me, Gage. Gage Patterson." He stuffed his phone in his back pocket. "My old man is here, and I think he's having a heart attack. You are Lacey Barnes, right?" He cocked his head and looked me dead in the eyes. Jesus, they were so sexy and dark, the color of chocolate. My knees shook, and I placed my hand on the desk for balance. I didn't want to deal with this. I opened my mouth to deny it, then noticed another nurse staring at us with curious eyes.

"Yes, I'm Lacey Barnes." I choked out. What the hell? I couldn't even act normal around him.

"Don't you remember me? We both attended the same school, we, um…" Gage said, and I saw a flush creeping up from the collar of his shirt to his tanned cheeks, covered in day-old stubble, the kind of stubble that instantly turned me on. My heart raced, and I felt beads of sweat forming on my upper lip. What the hell could I say? How did I escape his intense gaze without looking like a total moron? Images of me standing alone in front of hopeful and confused guests at my wedding flashed through my mind. I didn't want to hurt his feelings, but I'd had enough rejection lately to last an entire lifetime.

"Sorry, I can't talk right now."

Chapter Two

GAGE

"Damn it Gage, I will not get in the back of an ambulance, so don't call one." Dad barked, collapsing against the wall of the commercial building we were inspecting. He'd clutched his chest and gasped for air moments ago, and I'd immediately grabbed my phone.

"Dad, this could be serious." I jammed it back in my pocket. "Fine. If you're going to be stubborn, just get in the truck and I'll drive you home. Mom, can look after you. But don't you die on me, or she'll never speak to me again." I took Dad's elbow in my hand, which he shrugged off, lightly punching me in the shoulder. Then he straightened up and gingerly walked across the parking lot, at one point falling ever so slightly into a parked car. Once he was inside, he sat back in the seat and gasped for air. He was pasty looking, and his forehead was covered in a sheen of perspiration. I backed out of the lot and ran the stop sign at the end of the block.

"What the hell are you doing, boy? You'll get us killed!" Dad yelled, then gripped the oh-shit handle above the door. I said nothing and raced through every stop sign and traffic light on Capitol Boulevard, barrelling toward UNC Rex Hospital.

"Gage. Where are you driving me? You're going in the wrong direction." Dad panted, finally sounding like a man in distress.

"The hospital. Where the hell else would I take you?" I yelled, then instantly regretted it. Now that Dad knew where we were going, he'd make it harder for us to get there. I pulled into the parking lot of a grocery store then turned to face him.

"Listen, old man. You're going to the hospital whether you like it or not. Got it?" I could feel my pulse throbbing in my ears, and wondered if I was as difficult as my father with other people.

Dad reached for the door handle.

"Oh no you don't, you son of a bitch!" I stomped on the gas and pulled back onto the street, before Dad could open the door, narrowly missing two cars as I raced through a red light.

My father was a royal pain in the ass, but I'd rather have him alive than dead.

"Inky, don't talk to Mom yet. Dad's always been healthy, never had any issues with his heart. If it's serious, I'll call you." I paced in front of the nurses' station. My sister was freaking out almost as bad as I was, but I knew it wouldn't do any good to get Mom upset, unless it was a dire situation.

"I'm calling Erik and asking if he can fill in for me. I'll be right there." Her voice rose with every word, and then I heard the sound of breaking glass.

"What the hell was that?" Shit, I shouldn't have called her either. Between her and Mom, the entire hospital would be in an uproar in a matter of seconds.

"I fucking dropped a glass. I'm calling Erik now." She disconnected the call before I could stop her.

"Inky? Damn it." I was about to call her back when I saw a face I hadn't seen in years.

Lacey.

It couldn't be her. Maybe it was her doppelgänger, one of those lookalikes everyone was supposed to have. Of course, ten years had passed, and there were little differences. There was no way it could be her, but if it was, I had to speak. The only woman I'd ever loved was walking in the opposite direction, and I'd dreamt of seeing her again for a decade.

"Lacey?"

The woman stopped in her tracks, her back stiff, then slowly turned on her heels. Those bright green eyes met mine, and for a moment I couldn't breathe. Images of her soft curves and angelic face flushed with excitement while we made love flashed in my head. If it wasn't Lacey, it was her identical twin.

"May I help you?" She asked, then shifted her gaze from me to the floor. That was her voice, I knew it. Our friends used to tease her that she could make a living as a phone sex operator, because of how seductive she sounded.

"It's me, Gage. Gage Patterson. My old man is here, and I think he's having a heart attack. You are Lacey Barnes, right?" My heart galloped in my chest, and for a second I wondered if I'd be joining Dad in the examination room.

Lacey recognized me, I knew she did. Shit, I'd had so many conversations with her in my head over the years. When I was in the Marines she was by my side the entire time, even if it was only in my imagination. The memory of her smooth and sensual voice made the loneliness of Parris Island bearable, and those months in Afghanistan less horrifying.

"Yes, I'm Lacey Barnes." She placed her hand against the desk and peeked up again, not entirely meeting my gaze. I stepped forward, wanting to close the gap between us.

"Don't you remember me? We went to the same school, we, um…" I started, but I saw Lacey closing herself off, like an invisible forcefield slamming down between us.

"Sorry, I can't talk right now." Lacey's emerald eyes avoided mine

This couldn't be happening. How could she not want to talk, or even worse, what if she didn't remember me at all? Was Lacey hit on the head or something? Maybe did too many drugs at Harvard? Harvard, yes. I knew she went there, at the same time as I joined the Marines.

"You went to Harvard. I remember you were going to Florida, and then Harvard after graduation. I enlisted in the Marines. Dad made me... shit. My old man. Can you help me with him?" Fuck. If she was deliberately ignoring me, I'd at least get her to speak with me about Dad. Hell, what was I thinking, using my sick father to get at my high school crush at a time like this?

"Frank Patterson, yes, I've already seen him. He should be with Dr. Nash right now." Lacey said, then she grabbed a chart off the counter and glanced through it. She turned the sheets of paper over with her long tapered fingers, and then I noticed something. Her hands were trembling.

Lacey remembered me, she had to.

"Why don't I go check on him now. He was about to get an EKG when I left him. It shouldn't be long. Heart patients are always seen first." Lacey smiled, then placed the clipboard under her arm. She began walking off and then she turned around, took a deep breath and locked her hypnotic eyes with mine.

"Yes, I attended Harvard." She ran her fingers through her strawberry-blonde hair, then continued. "Let me check on your father now. Maybe we can chat a little more when we know how he's doing."

I paced the waiting room, resisting the urge to scream. My father could be dying, and the only woman I'd ever loved barely recognized me. Between these two events happening simultaneously, I thought I'd combust, my heart being shredded by the most important people I'd known in my entire life.

How could Lacey forget about me? And if she remembered, how come she'd pretended she didn't? That last evening we spent together still brought on an attack of the blues whenever I'd had too much to drink. It was a rare occurrence when I allowed that far-off memory to invade my brain, because it was so fucking painful. When she twisted the door handle to let herself out of the car for the final time, I wanted to pull her back inside and floor it. Harvard and the Marines could go to hell.

Pressure built behind my eyes, heat spreading to my cheeks. I knew I would blubber like a baby any minute now if I didn't calm down. I'd cried the night Lacey and I separated, torn apart by family obligations and an unfair world, and it hadn't happened since then. I balled my fists and placed them against my eyes, hoping to stem the tide. Moments later I heard footsteps, then felt a hand on my shoulder. When I looked up, Lacey was staring down at me. She raised one eyebrow the same as she used to do, then a genuine smile spread across her face. I always wondered how people could do that, only lifting one eyebrow at a time. She sat next to me and spoke in low measured tones.

"Your father is with Dr. Nash right now. Other than that, I don't have any information. I am the triage nurse, so all I did was check him in and make sure he was seen immediately. As soon as I know anything else, I'll tell you." Lacey placed her hands on the arms of the chair to push herself up and without thinking I seized her tiny wrist. Lacey sucked in her breath, then fell back in the seat. When I let go, she pressed her full lips together and opened her mouth. Initially, nothing came out, and I could see she was struggling to find the right words.

"You shocked me, that's all. I'm sorry Gage, but so much time has passed. Yes, I remember you, but… an awful lot has happened over the years. I don't know what else to say, but I apologize for not…" She stopped, then stood up, and this time I kept my hands to myself. Lacey glanced around the waiting room, then crouched down in front of me.

"This is not the time nor the place to talk about our past, about what might or might not have happened all those years ago. What I can say is that your father is receiving excellent care. I promise you that." She glanced at her watch. "I have to go upstairs and will be passing the cafeteria. Can I get you a cup of coffee perhaps, or a soda?" Warmth radiated from her now, instead of the cold woman I'd first encountered. I wanted to speak, but something held me back. I shook my head and crossed my arms over my chest. Lacey walked halfway across the waiting room, then stopped. It looked like she would turn around, but then she kept going.

Lacey was still gorgeous, regal, with curves in all the right places, and underneath her scrubs I could tell little had changed since we'd parted. But, she was right. Dad was sick, and this wasn't the right moment to stroll down memory lane.

My jaw clenched, frustration seeping into my bones. Why now? Couldn't I have run into her at a bar, or at the grocery store? This was torture, seeing Lacey after all these years while my father might be fighting for his life.

"No matter what happens, you and I need to talk, Lacey."

"Your father is asking for you. Follow me."

An older woman led me to a semi-private room where I found Lacey and the doctor, both with their arms crossed, and that wide-eyed gaze I'd come to recognize when Dad was tearing someone a new asshole. He stopped harassing them and turned his vitriol on me.

"I told you I would be all right. It wasn't a damned heart attack. This was the stupidest waste of time I've…"

I cut him off before his language became more exotic.

"Dad, if it had been you would've died. What the hell did you want me to do? Let you croak in the parking lot?" My pulse raced, and for the second time that day I wondered if I would be admitted to the hospital too.

"Your son did the right thing, Mr. Patterson. Plus, you aren't out of the woods healthwise. You have an ulcer, and I believe it's a result of stress. I am instructing you to cut down your workload, optimally taking a few days off. Maybe you could have your son help you with…" Dr. Nash began, then Dad shouted.

"Yeah, right, me take time off? No one in my real-estate firm is competent enough to do the shit I do. The business would go under in less than a week." Dad snarled, then glared at me with scarcely hidden contempt.

Fuck you, Dad.

The words were on my tongue, but I controlled myself. Lacey stared at me with what looked like pity, with a dash of horror thrown in. Damn it all, why did my father have to say this crap in front of her?

The old man had never given me any credit for the effort I put into making the company the success it was. This had been happening since day one, and the thought of walking away from the family business was always with me. I'd started my own real estate business on the side, hoping to back out of my father's firm gracefully, but I still worked with him part-time. Damn it, now I'd have to be with him more often to make sure he didn't overdo it.

Silence settled over us for a few moments, and finally, Dr. Nash spoke, "Mr. Patterson, I will have the nurse release you. She will give you information about a healthier eating plan, stress reduction techniques, and a prescription. I want to reiterate something though, and I'm being deadly serious. You must work on your stress levels. This ulcer is only the beginning of potential health problems, and if you don't address it now, you could very well end up back here with…"

"Yeah, yeah, yeah. Get me out of here, Gage," Dad barked, then swung his legs over the side of the bed. "Fetch that stuff from the nurse while I get dressed."

Lacey and the doctor left, and I trotted behind them,

grateful to escape the room. Once we were in the hallway, both spun around and faced me.

"You've got your hands full there. Please, do whatever you can to settle him down." The doctor gave me a rueful smile, and looked at Lacey. "This is your first day here, right?" Lacey nodded. "Welcome to the wonderful world of the ER. Never a dull moment." With that, he hurried off.

Lacey shrugged her shoulders and leaned against the wall, then she hung her head and laughed.

"Your father hasn't changed one bit. I'm sorry."

"Yeah. He's something else... Hey! You do remember stuff about us." I stood next to her on the wall, pressing my shoulder against hers. I wanted to wrap my arms around her tiny waist and pull her in tight. The feeling overwhelmed me, and I couldn't look Lacey in the eye. No one had ever replaced her in my heart, despite years of solitude and filling my bed with nameless strangers. If she still affected me this way, I needed to act on it, otherwise I'd always wonder what could have happened if I'd only spoken up.

"Can I take you to lunch tomorrow? If you're not busy or anything? I mean, I would like us to catch up. Nothing serious, no pressure. All I want is…"

"That would be nice." Lacey murmured, then I felt her shoulder leaning heavier into mine. I turned my head in her direction, and that goofy half-smile, the one she used to hide her feelings with, was there. Lacey had always been shy, and getting her to open up, to laugh and be herself was my mission in life when we were in high school. My heart lurched, and I wanted to run my fingers through her wavy blonde hair. I remembered doing that, always rubbing on her, touching her when I thought no one was looking.

"Gage! C'mon, get me out of here." Dad said, standing

in the doorway. Lacey pushed herself off the wall and jogged to the nurses' station. She found the papers we needed, and hurried back, handing Dad his release forms. Dad snatched them out of her hand and raced toward the exit.

"I got your number off his papers. I'll text you tomorrow." Lacey turned, flashed her brilliant white smile at me one last time, and rushed away.

I dashed off a text to Inky telling her Dad was heading home, that there was nothing to worry about, then he barked at me, "Gage! Jesus Christ, come on."

I shook off Dad's words and followed him out the exit. As I hustled after him, a bolt of anxiety shot through me, making my stomach clench, and I stopped for a moment, provoking a glare from the Old Man. A disquieting thought passed through my mind.

Had Lacey ever dreamed about me the way I did her?

Chapter Three

LACEY

"Want to eat with me in the cafeteria?" Powell asked as we walked off the floor of the ER.

I was torn. It would be so much easier to text Gage and tell him I couldn't make it for lunch. Powell was safe, a pleasant distraction from the crazy world of the ER. But, a promise was a promise, and I wouldn't let Gage down. Plus, I was curious about how his life had been since we parted ten years ago.

"I wish I could, but I've already got plans." I hurried out before Powell could try to persuade me otherwise. Gage and I were meeting at The Raleigh Times, an old restaurant that had existed since the earth cooled. It was a neutral place to meet up, and it had been years since I'd last eaten their fantastic Reuben sandwich.

"This would be so much easier if we'd met six months from now." I said aloud as I entered the parking deck and hustled toward my car. This wasn't part of my plans, meeting up with Gage, or any man, so soon after moving back to Raleigh. Gage was my high school boyfriend, that was all, nothing more, nothing less. I needed to look toward the future, and ex-boyfriends, hell, all men were not a part of it, even if Gage was still easy on the eye. But I'd be damned if I would give in to it. I'd had enough romance and rejection to last a lifetime, thank you very much.

I let myself in the car and was about to pull out of the deck when an image of our first kiss flashed through my mind. He'd always been the cocky kid in school, self-assured and used to getting his own way. When he showed an interest in me, I'd been shocked. Why was the most popular boy in our class suddenly following me around, determined to go out with me? I was the geeky girl whose face was always in a book.

It all started when a teacher asked me to help him with his classwork. We met in the library every day for a week, and to his credit, he kept his hands to himself. This made me believe he was just being friendly, that he truly was only looking to bring up his grades.

Then, he asked me to go with him to the prom. It was like a dream come true, having the handsomest guy in class ask me, shy, nerdy me out on a date, and to the prom where everyone would see us together. He'd been the perfect gentleman, holding my hand and making me feel like the most important girl on earth. And when we slow-danced together, I totally swooned in his arms.

For the next month we dated, and Gage *still* kept his hands to himself, until I began to wonder why he wasn't making any advances. So, I made the first move, asking him to take me to his room when his folks weren't at home. It was scary, because I'd never been with a man before, but at the time I was totally consumed by Gage, and couldn't imagine anyone else being my first.

Gage wasted no time, pushing me flat on my back against his bed, and covering my trembling body with his own. The heat I felt when his lips touched mine for the first time was something I'd never forgotten. He'd had a thick beard even then, and his stubble left my lips red and raw.

I loved it.

Neither of us knew what we were doing, instinct driving our lips to touch, and for our hands to fumble around awkwardly. Despite our lack of skills in the lovemaking department, he was an amazing lover, and I'd compared every man to him ever since. Most of them failed to measure up.

"Stop thinking about it now." I muttered to myself, and pulled onto the busy street. "Be positive." Gage was part of my past, and it might be worthwhile to catch up. I could use a friend, and he was probably only interested in that and nothing more. Reading anything else into this lunch date with an old boyfriend would be hazardous to my mental health.

Gage's larger-than-life presence always took over entire rooms, commanding the attention of everyone there. Standing on the sidewalk outside of The Raleigh Times, he seemed like the only person there, despite people maneuvering around him. He was well-over six feet tall, and wore tight red slacks and a crisp white button-down shirt that made his tanned skin glow. Damn it, why did Gage have to be my exact type? I tripped when we finally were face-to-face, and for a second I thought I'd end up on the ground. Instead, Gage caught me by the shoulders with a laugh.

"Thanks for coming." Gage grinned, then instead of

sticking his hand out to shake mine, he pulled me into an embrace. The feel of his warm muscular body pressed so close shocked me, and it transported me back to those long afternoons we'd spent in his bedroom after school. Heat radiated between my legs, then Gage's arms tightened. This was no quick hug between friends. The urge to melt into his enormous arms was overwhelming, but I knew nothing good could come of it.

Gage always had the ability to make me do whatever he wanted, whether it was skipping a class, or taking me in his bed. Now my body betrayed me, and I felt the old familiar excitement building inside, so I pushed back just the tiniest bit, enough for him to know to disengage. When Gage pulled away, I glanced at my watch.

"I don't have too long before I have to be back at work. Let's grab a table." I opened the door to the restaurant, grateful to see there wasn't a line to be seated. Moments later, a waitress led us to a booth in the back. Gage took the seat facing the dining room, while I was confronted with only him. I knew ten years had passed, but aside from building up his muscles, his face was almost the same. I noticed a few flecks of gray in his hair, but it made him more distinguished. If anything, he looked hotter than he did back then.

How long has it been since you had mind-blowing sex, Lacey? Or any sex at all?

"The special is the Reuben, and I highly recommend a bowl of the matzo ball soup too." The waitress interrupted my trance, and I sighed with relief. Looking up, I noticed Gage's gaze planted squarely on my face. A shiver coursed through me, and I turned away.

"That, um, that sounds great. I'll have both." I said, then Gage nodded. The waitress didn't see his nod and glanced at the tables surrounding us. I could see her impatience building, so I gave him a little kick under the table.

"I'll have what she's having." Gage's eyes never left mine as he spoke. I felt blood rushing up my neck, so I picked up the napkin and spread it across my lap, anything to avoid staring into his intense dark eyes. The waitress scurried away, and for a moment I wished she'd come back, to act as a buffer of some sort between us. How he made me feel so uncomfortable, so turned on after all these years was mystifying.

"Penny for your thoughts?" Gage said, his grin fading as I looked into his eyes once more. I obviously wasn't going to tell him I wanted to leap over the table and play ride 'em cowboy. Instead, I thought back to the questions I'd rehearsed last night in front of the mirror. I didn't want him to get the wrong idea. Nothing too intimate, but enough to let him know I was curious about his life since we'd parted.

"Well, I was wondering about what you've been up to since we last saw each other. You went into the Marines, right?" I asked, then Gage looked away for a second, and ran his fingers through his hair. He frowned, and I wondered if perhaps his life hadn't gone as well as he expected.

Before I could say something else, you know, to change the subject and lighten the mood, he spoke, "Yeah, at the end of our last summer together I went to Parris Island for boot camp. It was the most miserable I've ever been in my life. I wanted to be anywhere but there, but you know, sometimes you've got to do things you don't like. I'd like to think I made the best of it." Gage's eyes blanked for a moment. "Then, they sent me to Afghanistan. I'd only signed up for four years, but the war extended my stay by an extra fifteen months. It would have been longer, but I was injured, so they let me out."

"I hope it was nothing serious? What did you do next?" I imagined the worst, then briefly wondered how I would have reacted if we'd stayed in touch. How would I have felt finding out he was in a war zone, injured?

"Nothing too bad, hit by shrapnel. I have a scar on my back from it, but the war itself damaged my head more than the physical stuff. Seeing your buddies explode in front of you will shake your belief in, well, just about anything." Gage's eyes got smaller, and I felt my body responding to his words. Now I really wanted to wrap my arms around him. I struggled for the words to distract him, but he continued before I could spit something out.

"I came home and Dad put me to work. You've seen Dad at his worst, but he was at his best then. He knew I needed to keep busy, to put that time behind me. His answer to everything is work. At first I did maintenance, repairing plumbing, landscaping for our tenants, that kind of stuff. Then, he taught me how to open my own real-estate business, which I run when I'm not working for him. Now, when I look back at that period of my life, I am damned grateful to him for keeping me sane. Dad didn't give me the time to feel sorry for myself." He picked up his glass of water and sipped it, glancing away. Gage never liked to talk about himself from what I remembered. So why was he sharing so much? It wasn't like we knew each other that well anymore. This conversation was so heavy, not at all what I imagined it would be.

"What about you? How did Harvard treat you?" As soon as he asked me about school, the waitress brought our soup. I was embarrassed about that period of my life, and wondered if I should come clean about it. I looked up to see Gage waiting for me, the matzo ball soup untouched. Well, if he could be that open about his past, so could I.

"They threw me out." I said, then picked up my spoon and played with the soup, feeling more vulnerable than I thought I would.

"What are you talking about? I mean, you were the valedictorian of our class. I don't get it. What happened?" Gage said, his eyes wide.

"My roommate's boyfriend happened. He came on to me, and when I didn't respond to his advances, he got even by framing me for academic dishonesty. That's a fancy way of saying he accused me of cheating. I was tossed out, and after a year of waiting tables, I decided if I couldn't go to Harvard, I could at least get more education. I put myself through state college, and though I didn't become a doctor like I'd planned, I still got my nursing degree." I shrugged my shoulders. "Life doesn't always go the way we think it will, does it?"

Moments later our sandwiches arrived, and for a few minutes we said nothing as we consumed our lunch. I'd told no one about Harvard, about the embarrassment I felt at being kicked out of school. Why I'd felt the urge to share it with him, I didn't know. I snuck a few glances at him while we were eating. He still had that self-assuredness that compelled me to share everything with him, no matter how much it made me cringe. He was the only person who'd ever made me feel so open, comfortable.

"It's amazing you pulled yourself together after that." Gage said, interrupting my inner monologue. "So what brought you home, back to Raleigh?"

Damn it, the one question I didn't want to answer, especially to him. I thought back to the night before when I'd paced my room wondering what I'd say if he asked me about my move home. Yes, I'd stick with that explanation. The truth would be a little too revealing.

"The thought of another Boston winter was killing me. My parents live in Florida now, and I didn't want to go that far south, so this seemed like a good place to settle." I took a bite of my sandwich, unable to look him in the eye. For some reason the Reuben didn't taste as good as I remembered.

"What's the real reason you moved back?" Gage said, then bit his lower lip.

Damn it, why did he do this to me? I put the remnants of the sandwich on the plate and pushed it aside. All thoughts of discretion and common sense left me.

"I was engaged to be married to a doctor at the hospital I worked at. His name is Joseph, and he's a surgeon at Tufts. We'd planned the perfect wedding on the Cape, and most of the staff we worked with were attending. We were going to honeymoon in Barbados, and we'd already decided to buy a summer place in the Berkshires. I showed up in my Vera Wang gown, ready to say I do. He didn't." I bit off the last two words, surprised I still felt bitter. I'd discovered, much to my relief, how little it mattered to me. The affection I'd felt for Joseph wasn't love. It had been about status, and a reprieve from the loneliness which had crept up over the years.

"Joseph went on the honeymoon, but instead of me he took a surgical intern named Carrie. I hope they enjoyed themselves." I chuckled, surprising myself. Gage's mouth was open, and instead of being embarrassed, I felt a weight lifted from my shoulders.

"Honestly, I would have stayed in Boston if not for the gossip. Every day I'd go into work to find another rumor circulating throughout the hospital. Finally, I'd had enough and put in my notice."

"Damn, that's harsh. What an asshole. Count your lucky stars, Lacey You can do a lot better than that." Gage said, then he pushed his plate aside and leaned back in the booth. "I've avoided love, never wanted to put myself through the shit I see my friends putting up with. What I realized after you left, I'd never found the right woman. I mean, at the time, hell, I'm…" His words stumbled out of his mouth, and a blush came to his cheeks. His fingers tapped on the table, a staccato rhythm that gave away his embarrassment.

Suddenly, his face underwent a transformation, his lips curving up slightly. "What do you remember about us? You know, about our relationship?" Gage asked, then leaned forward waiting for my answer.

What the hell could I say? Yes, I'd spent a lot of time wondering how it would have worked out if I hadn't moved away to school, and if he hadn't joined the Marines. Gage was the only man who was able to get me to escape my head, and the insecurities, and make me feel... important? When he'd said he loved me the night we said goodbye, his words wrapped around me in an almost physical sensation, caressed and encircled by raw emotion. But after Joseph, and the humiliation of being dumped in the most visible way possible, I wasn't setting myself up for more disappointment.

"We were kids, discovering ourselves for the first time. I'll always remember it, in a good way."

Gage's face fell, the smile fading from his lips. Damn it, now I wanted to take it back, tell him how I'd really felt all those years ago. If only he knew how I'd spent years going on date after date, and being miserably disappointed in every man I saw. No one compared to his memory, but that was all he was now. Too much time had passed for him to be anything else, and I wasn't emotionally prepared for him to be anything more than a friend.

"So now I'm staying with my Aunt Millie until I find my own place." I said, breaking the awkward silence threatening us again. Gage's face lit up, and something in my gut loosened. I didn't like seeing him sad, especially if I'd caused it.

"Well, I'm just the man you need to see. I am a realtor, and I've got lots of places I could show you. Do you want to live downtown? I've got places in every price range, and I'd love to help you out." Gage said, nearly bouncing in his seat.

Damn, the energy he had reminded me so much of when we were teenagers. I had the urge to stroke the thick dark stubble covering his cheeks. In that moment I remembered exactly how he'd felt holding me, his full lips covering mine. This effect he had on me wasn't good, and I felt beads of sweat forming on my upper lip.

"Are you ready for your check?" The waitress didn't wait for our answer and placed it on the table before rushing to the next one.

Thank God.

"I've got this." Gage said, snatching it up in his large calloused hand before I could grab it.

"You don't have to do—" I started, before he interrupted.

"Yes, I do, but you have to do me a favor." He said, light dancing in his eyes. Damn, his eyelashes were still so thick, like he wore eyeliner, though I was sure he didn't. "Lacey...? You still there?" Fuck, he'd caught me staring.

I shook my head and laughed. "Sorry, I have a lot on my mind with my new job, trying to find a place to live. You know." I shrugged my shoulders, hoping to play it off.

"Well, I want you to come and see me. I've got time later

this afternoon to show you a few places. I mean, you do need a place to live. What time do you get off? Work, I mean, when do you get off work?" He dipped his head down while keeping his gaze focused on me. I blurted out the time before I could think of an excuse not to.

"5:30."

"Excellent." Gage glanced at his watch and stood. "Sorry to eat and run, but I'll miss an appointment if I don't scoot." He placed his business card on the table in front of me, then laid his heavy hand on my shoulder. "See you later tonight."

"Yeah, I'll come by after work." I responded weakly, then Gage's face broke into that huge grin I'd never forgotten, the one that made me squirm inside. Damn it. Moments later I heard the bell on the door of the restaurant ring as he let himself out.

"What the hell are you doing?" I grumbled to myself, clenching my fists, then I stood and chased him out the door. When I got to the sidewalk I scanned the street, hoping to catch him before he left. I wanted to cancel, tell him I couldn't make it, but I was too late.

"Gage, why do you do this to me?" I muttered, then hurried toward my car. When I got in I peered into the rear-view mirror, surprised to find myself grinning from ear to ear. He used to do this to me all the time when we were teenagers. He'd find a way of inviting himself over to my house, but making it seem like it was my idea, or how we'd suddenly be kissing and it was almost always me who initiated it.

"Establish boundaries. Don't give him the impression you want anything more than friendship. Oh, and a place to live."

Gage wanted to catch up, that was all. He didn't say anything to make me think otherwise, and had behaved like a perfect gentleman. Though something in his eyes made me think he wanted something more.

It was the way he looked at me with that self-assured grin and cocky attitude. Demanding the attention of everyone in a room, whether they wanted to give it or not. He was the eternal bad boy, used to getting whatever he wanted, all while looking as innocent as an angel.

"I'm not giving in this time, Gage." I whispered, then put my car in gear and headed back to the hospital.

Chapter Four

GAGE

"Gage, your four o'clock appointment cancelled." The receptionist poked her head through the door to say, then hustled back to her desk.

"Oh shit, I forgot I had one." I mumbled to myself, and leaned back in the chair, propping my feet on the desk.

My normal, bland world had faded away as soon as I'd laid eyes on Lacey again. Seeing her had provoked major butterfly action in my gut—something I hadn't felt for anyone since we parted ten years ago. That was cause for concern. I'd prided myself on being a lone shark in a sea of women, swooping in on my prey and getting what I wanted before pesky feelings developed in me, or my lover, for the night. As long as no one got hurt, of course.

"Simple, casual sex is what it's supposed to be, not this crap." I said aloud, grateful Dad wasn't here to see me in this state. As soon as I'd seen Lacey in the ER, I was lost again in those feelings I'd done my best to forget about. No one had ever broken through the cage I kept my heart locked up in.

I remembered the first day of my junior year in high

school, which was the first time we'd met. The catholic school we went to made girls wear the least attractive uniform possible, a plaid skirt and a boring white shirt. Despite the efforts of the nuns, Lacey's beauty shone through. We had just one class together, but the only thing I could focus on the entire day was her. I learned her name when the teacher called on her, and for the rest of the day and throughout the night it echoed in my head.

LaceyLaceyLaceyLaceyLaceyLacey

I tried to make eye contact with her during class, but she kept her eyes on her notes. For the entire fifty minutes of boring Latin she'd avoided my gaze, despite my willing her mentally to look in my direction. Hell, I even prayed for her to look at me. I was used to getting what I wanted, and it only spurred me on to make her my friend, and hopefully more.

I'd never been a quitter. Getting what I wanted was ingrained in my psyche. Not only was I stubborn, I was also infinitely patient when pursuing a goal. The way I got to Lacey the first time was by deliberately flunking a Latin test. I'd always gotten good grades which baffled my teacher, so she asked Lacey to help me with my classwork. She was the new kid, and she made excellent grades, so I figured she'd pair us together. Lacey would make a new friend, and help me get my grades up. At the time I was only guessing this strategy would work, but my instincts were spot on.

The third time we met in the library to study together was when I made my first move. The moment she laid her books down next to mine, the air in the room shifted, becoming electric. I'd looked up to her and smiled, gratified to see a blush creeping up her neck until her cheeks flushed pink. Lacey pulled out her notes from class, but I had no use for them and laid my hand on hers for a brief moment, then pulled it away.

"We are here to study, right?" Lacey stuttered, her bright green eyes growing wide.

"What is something you've never told a soul about?" I asked, delighted to see the effect it had on her. Lacey's eyes scanned the room. We were sitting in the back of the stacks at a table reserved for studying. There was no one else around.

"Why are you asking me that? Aren't we supposed to be conjugating Latin verbs?" Lacey whispered.

"Come on, I'll tell you a secret if you share one with me." I leaned into her arm as I said it, wanting to put her at ease.

"If it'll make you want to study, then… fine. I count stuff in my head all the time."

"What do you mean?" I asked.

"Like, if I'm walking to class, I count all of my steps in my head, or if I'm eating, I count how many times I chew my food. I know it's strange, but…" Lacey shrugged, then turned and gazed into my eyes. "Your turn."

My eyes dropped to her full pink lips, and the urge to cover them with my own struck me. I gripped the sides of my chair to keep my paws to myself. Unable to think of anything to confess, my mouth stayed shut. Finally, Lacey elbowed me in the side, and grinned.

"C'mon, fair's fair. Tell me a secret."

"Okay, um…" I wracked my brain for something. I'd only asked her for a secret to get her to talk. It never occured to me that I'd need to confess something too.

"Whenever I read a book, this is in private of course, I act out the scenes, speaking the different parts aloud like I'm on stage, or in a movie. I use different voices and mannerisms for each character." I blushed, but didn't know why. It wasn't like I told her that I jerked off twice, sometimes three times a day. That was a pervy secret I'd take to my grave.

"Gage, what the hell is happening with the Granger deal?" Dad barged into my office, startling me from my memories. He perched on the edge of my desk, frowning. I swung my feet to the floor and sighed.

"Dad, I sent the owner of the apartments an offer, the exact one you told me to. I still haven't heard from him." I replied, inwardly cringing, because I knew what would happen next.

"Donald is a friend of the family." Dad bellowed, then hit the top of the desk with his fist. "He's also one of our best clients. He wants to buy that property, and he's got more than enough money to make the owner a deal he can't refuse. Call him, go see him in person, I don't care. Make this deal happen, or I'll be very disappointed in you. Again." He said the last word through clenched teeth, then stalked out of my office in search of someone else to harass.

Fuck my life.

Dad had a talent for making me feel pathetic. Here I was boasting to myself about getting anything I wanted, and he had the power to make me feel like I was a stupid kid. If only he believed in me, trusted that I knew what I was doing. It wasn't like I didn't want us to succeed. The commission on this deal alone would make me a huge chunk of change. Screw it, focus on what you really want.

Lacey.

I glanced at my watch. She'd be here in a few minutes, and I hoped Dad would make an early night of it. I wanted nothing to spoil my time with Lacey, but if anyone could, it would be Dad. I'd put a folder together with different condos for sale, hoping I'd get to show her a few in person. Perhaps I could take her out for a drink afterward? Maybe, if I played my cards right, she'd let me hold her again, kiss her like I did the very first time?

"You have the entire basement to yourself?" Lacey asked as I led her down the stairs. I'd told her we were going to play video games, and maybe we would, eventually.

"Yeah, my sister's at boarding school, so most of the time it's all mine."

I realized I'd somehow have to walk her through the TV room, which had the video games prominently displayed, in order to get her to the bedroom. That might not prove to be easy.

"Oh cool, you get to play on a large screen TV?" Lacey gushed, and started toward the sofa in front of the television.

"It's pretty cool, but I want to show you something else first." I grabbed her by the elbow and steered her down the hallway to my bedroom. Finally, I'd see if what I was feeling for Lacey was mutual. I took a deep breath and opened the bedroom door. I wasn't going to let fear stop me, though I knew the consequences could be harsh. My blood pumped faster, adrenaline coursing through my veins. Lacey stood in front of my bed, one eyebrow raised. At that moment I knew this was right.

"What are you doing?" Lacey placed shaking hands on my chest as if she wanted to push me back. I placed my hands on her shoulders and pushed ever so slightly until the backs of her knees were against the edge of the mattress.

"I'm doing what you want, what I've wanted since I first laid eyes on you Lacey."

One final push and she fell back against the mattress and I covered her with my body. Gazing into her eyes, I gave her one last chance to say no.

"Stop me now if you don't want this."

Her innocent face gave the faintest of nods, and moments later my lips crashed into hers. The jolt of her soft mouth pressed against mine made me forget anything else existed. I wasn't sure what to do, and let instinct guide me, though I was fairly sure I needed to keep all the action above the neck, though the feel of her breasts heaving underneath me was driving me crazy.

I licked her lips, urging them to open, and when our tongues first touched, a groan rumbled through me, and she whimpered in response. My cock was so fucking hard, painfully hard, and the only relief came from pushing it against her. It was a throbbing I'd never felt before, so intense I thought I'd pass out.

"What are you doing to me? Oh God, Gage, I've wanted this since the day we first met." Lacey said as she broke away from our first kiss. Her hand reached out and grasped the back of my head, then pulled my face back toward hers…

The receptionist cracked my door open. "Lacey Barnes is here to see you." She held the door open as Lacey walked in, then she shut it behind her. She stood in front of my desk, not saying anything, her green eyes dancing around my office.

This was my first time seeing her in regular clothes, not her hospital uniform, and my hunch had been correct. Beneath the shapeless scrubs was the same curvy body I'd fallen for years ago. Her jeans appeared to be glued on, hugging her hips, and a green tank top barely concealed her perfect tits. Plus, they made her eyes positively glow. Lacey's pale skin had a smattering of freckles on her shoulders, and I wanted to lick them. My cheeks warmed, and I realized I had to break the silence before it became overwhelming.

"So, this is where the magic happens." I laughed awkwardly, standing up. I didn't know whether to hug her, shake her hand, or pull her into my arms and kiss her the way I used to do. Instead of making a fool of myself, I gestured toward the seat in front of the desk. Then Dad poked his head through the door. He took a long look at Lacey, then at me.

"You're bringing the hospital to me now?" He said, scowling. I shook my head, hating every second of Dad's scorn.

Lacey's mouth dropped open, then she spoke, "No worries Mr. Patterson. I'm here to find a place to live." Lacey glanced in my direction.

I was about to say something I'd regret, but the emerald green of her eyes stilled my tongue. I looked up to see Dad smiling for a change.

"Good, good. We have excellent properties for you to choose from, and the best prices in the city. Oh, Gage, remember what I told you about the Granger deal. I need it taken care of pronto." Dad said, then shut the door quietly as he left. Whenever money was being exchanged, he switched from being a devil to an angel, lickety split.

Lacey laughed, then bit her lip to quiet it.

"As you see, he hasn't changed a bit." I guffawed, then moments later both of us were holding our sides, unable to contain ourselves. It felt so fucking awesome, like we were teenagers pulling one over on our folks again, breaking curfew, or sneaking a kiss goodbye. Her laughter was like gold, and then it struck me that this was the first time I'd heard her really laugh since she'd re-entered my life. I'd give anything to keep Lacey this way, carefree, playful and happy.

Moments later though, Lacey sobered up and a look of purpose replaced her smile.

"So, what do you have to show me?"

I opened the folder on my desk and spread the different brochures in front of her, deliberately keeping a specific listing on top of the others.

"You didn't give me an idea of the area you want to live in, so I've got a few properties in mind. Are you looking to buy or rent? Did you know what part of the city you want to live in? Or did you want to look a little further out, like in Wake Forest, or Durham?" I asked.

"I'd rather be close to work, so downtown would be perfect. I hate driving, so someplace close enough I could catch the bus, perhaps? Oh, and I still don't know if I want to stay in Raleigh permanently, so I think a rental would work best." Lacey picked up the brochure I'd laid on top.

I had to look away, so she couldn't see the look of disappointment I felt when she said she wanted to rent. I wasn't stupid, and I knew enough time had passed that maybe she wasn't attracted to me anymore, but I didn't like the sound of her leaving again. Damn it, I wanted a chance to discover if the way I felt was real, not some stupid fantasy.

"Why don't we look at some of the rentals in person? The brochures don't really do them justice, know what I mean?" I said.

"Sure, as long as you don't mind driving. So much has changed around here. I almost got lost on the way to your office." Lacey grinned, and my heart flipped in my chest.

"Pick out the ones you're interested in while I grab the

master keys from the back." I stood, and when I passed behind her, I couldn't help myself and squeezed her shoulder. Lacey's back stiffened for a moment, then she relaxed. My heart started beating again, and I hustled out of the office. When I closed the door I fell against the wall, regretting that slip. I didn't want to scare her off, and moving too fast was the easiest way to do just that.

"Keep your cool Gage, don't lose control." I whispered, then glanced up to see the receptionist eyeing me with a raised brow.

What the hell was wrong with me? It was like I had some weird gene leftover in me from the caveman days. Just being close to her made me crazy, losing every ounce of self-control I possessed. I pushed myself off the wall and ran down the hallway to get the keys out of the closet where we had them hanging on hooks. I raced back, then realized I'd be out of breath and I needed to chill out for a moment. Once I got my breathing under control, I let myself back into the office.

"See any apartments you're dying to look at?" I grinned, hoping she'd picked the one on top.

"Yes, I think I'm interested in one of these." I took the brochures from her hand and bit my lip to keep from smiling.

"Your wish is my command. Let's go."

"I love this place." Lacey breathed, her footsteps echoing on the hardwood floors. Her eyes were glued to the balcony overlooking Fayetteville Street. She slid open the screen door and stepped outside. Dusk was approaching, and the sky was streaked with orange and purple clouds. I stood next to her, resisting the urge to put my arm around her waist.

"Look down. Everyone on the street is so tiny from up here." I said, then noticed her gripping the railing tight. "Are you nervous about heights?"

"Oh, no. This view, wow. It's incredible. I really missed Raleigh. Why the hell did I stay away for so long?" She murmured, shaking her head.

I've been wondering the same thing.

"You can be at the hospital in ten minutes depending on traffic. If you don't want to drive, you can catch the bus two blocks away at Moore Square. The laundry room is at the end of the hallway, and there's a gym on the first floor. It's a happy place. Most of our tenants have been here for a long time. The only reason this unit opened up is the previous tenant got married and moved away. She'd been here for seven years if I remember correctly." I realized I was babbling and shut my trap. Let the surroundings sell her on the place.

Lacey had always been slow to warm up to things. When we first started hanging out, she'd been painfully quiet, but then slowly she'd come out of her shell. Once comfortable, Lacey would run her mouth, desperate to tell me her secrets, or talk about the weird insecurities we all had, but never felt comfortable sharing. I wanted that Lacey back, and the only way it would happen was for her to come to me.

"I'll take it." Lacey leaned into my shoulder as we stood against the railing of the balcony. I barely controlled the urge to jump up and down.

"Excellent decision. You're gonna love it here. Let's run back to my office, sign the lease and I'll give you the keys. You can move in as soon as you want." I said, wanting to grab her by the waist, spin her around and enfold her in my arms. Instead, I pushed myself off the railing and walked inside.

When I turned around to see if she was following, Lacey was less than a foot behind me, and we nearly collided. She backed up half-a-step, and that sexy blush started all over again, working its way up from her neck. Then she stunned me by reaching out and placing her hand on my shoulder.

"Since you bought me lunch, can I buy you dinner?" Lacey murmured, a small smile slowly stretching across her face. My mouth opened to reply, but nothing came out.

"Shit, I'm sorry, you've probably got other plans." She looked down at the floor and then started to walk around me toward the door. I reached out in the nick of time and grabbed her elbow.

"No, no no, I don't have any plans. I'd love to have dinner. We can go to Beasley's, they've got great fried chicken, and it's just down the street. I can show you around the neighborhood and stuff." I held my breath, not sure why, since she was the one who'd asked me out. Lacey's eyes locked with mine, and my legs felt weak.

Finally, she answered. "Let's go. I'm famished."

Chapter Five

LACEY

"Sign here, and here." Gage said, then laid the keys to my new apartment next to my hand. I picked them up, feeling a twinge of panic. Locked into a lease for a year, a commitment to stay in Raleigh for at least that length of time. Stuffing them in my pocket, I looked up to see Gage's huge sparkling grin, and for a moment I felt something I hadn't in a long time: hope. Maybe, just maybe, the dreams I'd had over the years about me and him could come true.

Tearing my eyes away from his, they dragged down his thick, muscled body. His white button-down shirt barely contained his massive pecs, and then his stomach flattened out before hitting the top button of his tight red slacks, and if my memory was accurate, underneath those buttons was an extra-large…

"Lacey? You okay?" Caught staring, I felt blood rushing to my face. I stood and backed away from the desk. Endorphins raced through my body, reacting to the unfamiliar giddy lust Gage was provoking in me. I wracked my brain for something to say, and settled on the truth. Well, minus the lustful thoughts.

"Sorry, I guess I'm going to be in Raleigh for a minimum of a year now. I never thought it would be home again. Kinda scary to tell you the truth." I shook my head, wondering why I'd told him that. It had always been like this with him, a special magic he had to extract every private thought in my head.

"Well, maybe that's not such a bad thing. Actually, it makes me want to celebrate. Ready for dinner?" Gage came around the desk and rubbed my lower back, the heat of his hand soothing, almost hypnotic, like his deep, gravelly voice. I could feel our off-the-charts chemistry rising to an incendiary level. A groan worked its way up my throat, and I felt myself getting wet from his touch, so I coughed and backed away.

"Definitely. I've eaten nothing since lunch and I'm starving. I'll take my car and follow along behind you." I said, then raced out the door before he noticed what his hands did to me. Gage's touch drove me crazy, firm and strong, and would persuade me to do things I wasn't sure I was ready for.

When I sat my car, it struck me that it had been months since I'd last had sex—with Joseph, of course—and what I didn't admit at that time was how I occasionally fantasized about other men to enjoy it.

I'd give credit where credit was due; Joseph wasn't a bad lover. What had been missing was the deep connection I longed for, but could never quite manage with him. At the time I wrote it off to premarital jitters, or a fear of commitment. Maybe there was something more to it than I thought.

A horn beeped. Gage waved as he pulled his cherry-red pickup out of the lot. I drove behind him, and while sitting at a red light, it dawned on me that when I'd fantasized about other men while with Joseph, most of the time it was a burly, faceless dark-haired devil, similar to the one I was taking to dinner.

"The veggie sandwich is wonderful, and of course they are famous for their fried chicken and honey." Gage said as we opened our menus. The atmosphere was funky and eclectic, though Gage's taste in food surprised me. I thought he was into fitness and eating healthily.

"I'm surprised you'd like fried chicken and burgers, because it's obvious you're into working out, and I thought you'd be counting calories or eating low-carb." I asked, unable to tear my eyes away from his biceps. They were threatening to rip the sleeves of his shirt.

"Normally I eat healthy, but occasionally I like to indulge in food that actually tastes good. The smash burger is yummy, like a heart attack on a plate." Gage grinned, then his eyes met mine, faltered, and shifted back to the menu.

Damn, this man still took my breath away. Objectively speaking, I'd seen better looking men than Gage, but they were usually on the poster of the latest blockbuster movie, not someone you'd meet in real life. He was a stud, but it was his magnetic aura that drew me to him, and try as I might to resist, maybe I was being kinda silly about the whole thing?

"Gage, how've you been?" A tall man with dark hair and a shorter woman with fiery-red hair and a nose ring appeared at the table.

"Great, no complaints. This is my, um, an old friend from high school who just moved back to town, Lacey. Lacey, meet two of my favorite people, Marcy and Cameron." Gage introduced us, and for a split second I worried that they would sit at the table, which felt stupid once I thought about it. Gage and I were just friends, having a friendly dinner, and that was it. No reason for me to fear they would intrude.

"Do you guys want to join us?" Gage asked, then glanced in my direction. I shrugged my shoulders and grinned, praying they wouldn't.

"We just finished an early dinner. The babysitter can't stay late, because it's a weeknight, so we need to get home early. Oh, and Marcy has an interview in the morning for a job. Otherwise, we'd love to join you both. It was nice meeting you, Lacey." Cameron said, then winked at Gage before the two of them turned on their heels and left.

"They are good people, and they used to rent from me. Actually, Cam and Marcy live in a house I sold them three blocks from here. You're gonna like living in downtown Raleigh, lots of cool people in the area." Gage flashed that blinding smile again. It made me forget where I was for a second, but then I remembered to keep the conversation going.

"I remember as a kid that downtown was so empty, filled with abandoned old buildings. It's amazing how they've turned things around. Most of these businesses and restaurants weren't here when I left town ten years ago," I said.

"Well," Gage leaned back in his chair with a confident smirk."You can thank me for a lot of that. I started my real estate business buying those old buildings and fixing them up. I always saw potential here and knew we could bring the downtown district back. It's all about believing in yourself, making goals and doing whatever it takes to make it happen. You've done a pretty decent job of that yourself. What you told me about Harvard, and the shit that happened to you, most people would have folded, hightailed it and run away. You took the bull by the horns and made a career for yourself despite the odds. Shows you have guts and determination. I like that." Gage's grin flattened out, and I saw fire in his eyes.

My stomach flipped. How the hell could I resist him? Every time I saw him it hit me physically, made me want to, I didn't know… relive the past? My love life over the years had been sporadic at best, and the last time I'd committed myself to someone, he took off with a younger woman.

"Gage, I sent you a text yesterday and never heard back." A young woman in her early twenties was suddenly behind Gage and placed her hands on his shoulders in a very familiar way. Whoever she was, the woman appeared like she'd walked off the pages of a fashion magazine. Gage stiffened and glanced up to see who it was. He blushed, then leaned forward, so the hands slipped off him.

"Um, I've been busy. Work and stuff, you know, the usual." Gage put his face in his palms for a brief second, then looked up at the woman again, a look of confusion on his face. The stranger finally noticed me and frowned.

"Is this who you're doing now? Aren't you going to introduce us?" A hint of annoyance crossed the girl's pinched face. Gage reached across the table and took my hand in his, folding my fingers into his palm.

"This is Lacey." He stated, and I wished the ground would open up and swallow me. It felt like the entire restaurant was a stage, a spotlight over our table. I glanced around, wondering if every person there was focused on us. All I could think about was his hand holding mine, possessively sending a message to this woman that I was his, and to back off. Butterflies danced in my stomach. Then, a disturbing thought struck me. Was he only holding it to get rid of this obviously pissed-off girl?

"You can't even remember my name can you? Asshole." The woman turned to leave, then smirked in my direction. "Honey, he does this to all the girls. Don't think he won't do the same to you."

Her heels click-clacked across the dining room floor. When she got to the door she opened it and waved her manicured fingers in my direction, then she slammed it behind her.

So much time had passed, and I had to admit, that young girl might be a clue as to the type of man Gage really was. His eyes were gazing intently into mine. Memories flooded back of how we used to hold hands in his car, or at the movies. I remembered feeling like a fish out of water as a teenager, and how Gage's touch would ground me, make me feel accepted and loved for who I was. He'd always been full of himself, but underneath his self-assuredness was a kind man who lived to make me smile.

"I'm sorry about…" Gage began, then we were interrupted.

"What can I get for you this evening?" A waitress dressed head to toe in black asked, startling me. I pulled my hand away from Gage's and snatched up the menu. Inwardly, I thanked the woman for saving me. This man, who at one time was my reason for living, now scared the bejesus out of me.

"Thank you for dinner. Actually, I don't remember the food much, so I thank you for the company. I'm glad we're spending time together." Gage leaned against his truck door, his eyes trapping mine. "I know we're just getting to know each other again..." He paused between every word, "...but you must know, you mean more to me than just friends. I've never forgotten you, Lacey." Gage laced his fingers around the back of my neck. His scent, that woodsy scent that turned me on so damn much flooded my nostrils. A warm flush traveled down my neck to my chest, and my nipples perked up at his touch.

"Gage, you don't know how much I want to believe you." I sighed, then pulled him in close, inhaling his scent as I did. My heart was thumping, but I couldn't figure out why. Was it fear, or lust? A combination of the two? Christ, I was probably overthinking the whole thing.

"I want you to—"

Gage's voice cut off mid-sentence, and it was my fault. I was kissing him. The taste of his lips against mine was so familiar, yet new. More powerful than my memories of his youthful kisses, which drove me mad back then, and were doing so much more even now. The way he smelled and the texture of his thick stubble around my lips felt so damn right. I was drowning in a heaven I'd never really forgotten, pushed back into my memories by his lips and arms wrapped around me. Every nerve ending in my body was singing as I melted into his embrace.

Gage pulled back and took my face in his hands. A growl issued from his throat and then he crushed my mouth in another kiss. He tilted my head to the side and sucked on my tongue, then nibbled my bottom lip before it became a deep, passionate embrace that forced me to remember what his mouth felt like on other parts of my body. There was an urgency to it, as if we were making up for the time and distance that had kept us apart. Most importantly, it felt natural, like it was supposed to be just him and me holding each other up, the two of us against the world. It went on for what seemed like hours, but when it was over felt like mere seconds.

"Mmmm." Gage groaned, a heart-wrenching sound I remembered from years past, when we'd said goodbye.

Goodbye.

My God, what if he was just a player, hooking up with younger girls like that young woman at the table? What if he was like Joseph, pretending to love me while fucking his surgical assistant?

Gage could destroy me.

"What…? Why are you pushing me away?" Gage pleaded as I pushed him back. His mouth hung half open, and his arms reached for me as I backed away. "Please, I'll do anything to…"

"I'm... I'm sorry Gage. I shouldn't have kissed you." I whispered, shaking my head slowly. Of all the things that would send me into a tailspin, it would be Gage, leaving me and breaking my heart. He had that power, and it would destroy me in a way that would make Joseph's no-show at the altar seem like a minor blip in my timeline.

"I'm sorry." I stammered again, then I ran to my car. My hands trembled as I opened the door, my brain unable to catch up with my heart. Once I crashed into the seat, I attempted to slip the key into the ignition, but my hands were shaking too much. I took a few deep breaths, hoping to clear my head, then I looked out the window. Gage was leaning against his truck, his back to the street, shoulders shaking. I'd only seen him cry once, and that was the night we were forced to say goodbye. We were reliving that night ten years later, and it was my fault. As teenagers I'd never seen him show even a hint of weakness, always in control of his every emotion. Gage's strength was what drew me to him, but the fact that he'd lost it whenever I was involved, only made me want him more.

"What the hell have I done?" I groaned, then looked into the rear-view mirror, surprised to see streaks of black mascara sliding down my face.

"I'm happy you found a new apartment, sweetie, though you don't look terribly excited." Aunt Millie handed me a glass of chardonnay. She was my favorite relative, and I'd been grateful she'd taken me in while I found a place. We'd always had a strong bond, and though she was family, I truly thought of her as a best friend.

I wondered how much I could tell her about my evening. When I got to her house she'd immediately asked what was wrong. I'd shrugged it off, hoping to avoid any questions, but she'd always had a way of divining my moods, fishing out all the details I held back from everyone else.

"It's on Fayetteville Street downtown, that big apartment building with mirrored walls next to the Raleigh Savings And Trust building. I'm renting it from someone I knew in high school, Gage. We went to dinner after I signed the lease, and, well, things didn't go the way I thought they would." I sighed, not wanting to get into the particulars of the disastrous evening. The thing was, I needed to say something about it. I felt so uncomfortable, knowing I'd hurt him. Gage never cried. Don't ask me how I knew it, but I did.

"Gage? Do you mean that boy you were in love with in

high school?" Aunt Millie asked, a grin spreading across her rosy cheeks. I could tell she'd had more than one glass of wine. Normally, she wasn't this forthcoming.

"How...? How did you know? I never told you about him." I was flabbergasted.

"No dear, you never said a word about Gage. You didn't have to. But, I remember it like it was yesterday, that boy always following you. Whenever you came over to visit, he was there, tagging along. You were always smiling, which beat the hell out of the brooding teenager you were before you met him. It reminded me of how I felt about your Uncle Gordon. I never wanted him out of my sight. Damn, I miss him to this day." Aunt Millie's husband had died when I was young and she'd never remarried.

"So, why did you move back to Raleigh? Wasn't it to start afresh, to find new adventures? Because if there are any other reasons, you need to examine them. You should embrace life, not run away from it." She stated, locking her slightly blood-shot eyes to mine. As usual, she had a point.

"You know why I moved back to Raleigh." I waited for her to interject, and when she didn't, I continued. "Because of Joseph, and his dumping me for another woman. Being left at the altar wasn't my finest moment. I'm not ready to be with anyone. It's too soon."

"But you weren't really in love with him, were you?" She held up her glass, as if toasting herself for accurately figuring it all out when I couldn't.

She was right, of course, but I didn't want to even contemplate the misery I'd feel if I started something with the first, and possibly only, man I'd ever loved. If he betrayed me like Joseph had, it would destroy me. When Joseph abandoned me at the altar, it changed the way I thought about the world. I now distrusted everyone, regardless of how well I knew them. Even if I never felt for Joseph what I should have felt for a husband, the humiliation had never left me.

"No, I wasn't. That doesn't mean it didn't hurt though." I sighed. "I have to admit I felt a certain sense of, I don't know, relief? Part of me is glad that it didn't work out. The problem is, I messed things up tonight. It's just—" I started, but she interrupted me with questions I was too afraid to answer.

"Is Gage still in love with you?" She stared at me over her wine glass, an eyebrow lifted, then dropped the bomb.

"Are you still in love with him?"

Chapter Six

GAGE

"Honey, I have a meeting at the Garden Club, and then I'm getting fitted for the gown I'm wearing to the charity ball. Gage will take you to your doctor's appointment." Mom said. As usual, she was the only person capable of getting Dad to act like a somewhat reasonable person, though this morning the old man was putting up resistance.

"What the hell, Mary? I'm capable of driving myself. He needs to be closing the Granger deal." Dad glared at me. The breakfast room was painted bright yellow with red trim that Mom said was supposed to make everyone more cheerful in the morning. Feng shui? Whatever it was, its mystical powers were not working today.

"Frank, if I let you drive yourself you won't go. You'll end up at some greasy spoon and make your ulcer worse." She glanced at her watch impatiently, then noticed Dad's scowl. "This is not a request. Gage will take you to the appointment, but Trish will pick you up. She wants to take you to lunch. Now put your jacket on and scoot." She pecked him on the cheek, grabbed her purse and hurried out.

Mom refused to call my sister Trish by her nickname, Inky, and blissfully ignored the head to toe tattoos covering her. Living in a world of her own, my mother ignored what she didn't like and pretended that our family was perfect, as if we lived in a TV sitcom from the 1950s. I think that was why her marriage to Dad worked. She ignored his foul moods, and pretended he was the star of Leave it to Beaver.

"Good. She's gone. Now, this is what will really happen this morning."

"Shit." I groaned, then Dad carried on talking.

"You're going to take me to…" he grumbled, but was interrupted by Mom, who was standing at the door.

"Gage Scott Patterson, I'm going to wash your mouth out with soap! You know how much I hate the brown word. Frank, if you bully Gage into letting you cancel that appointment, you will regret it. Trust me on this. Now, get in his truck and go. I have too much to do to be babysitting you today." She kissed Dad on the cheek again, then pecked mine for good measure. "Don't let him get away with his usual nonsense. Oh, and watch your language." She wagged her finger at me, then left.

"You heard her, Dad, let's get this over with." I sighed, not in the mood to deal with his tantrums today. Usually I'd let the verbal abuse slide, knowing when to pick my battles, but since my disastrous night with Lacey, I rivaled Dad for the title of Grumpiest Man in Raleigh.

"Fine, I'll go." Dad snatched his jacket off the back of his chair and stomped out. I took a few deep breaths and followed behind, hoping Dad would keep his mouth shut for the ride, but knowing he wouldn't.

"I know I keep harping on about this, but the Granger deal is very important to me and the firm. We stand to make a great deal of cash if we can get that hippy to sell those apartments." Dad uttered, then swiped at his forehead with the back of his hand. I noticed something I'd never seen before, or perhaps didn't want to notice. Fear. He was afraid, and maybe it was his mortality that had him on edge instead of his usual bad temper.

"Dad, I am heading over to the Millbrook Arms Apartments to speak with Mr. Parker. If he refuses to budge, I'll offer him an additional ten percent, as long as Mr. Granger approves it." I said. We were waiting for his appointment with the internist at VCU Medical Center.

"Don't worry about Donald Granger. He'll pony up any amount of money to buy that dump. Never forget that Donald has been a loyal client since I opened the business almost forty years ago. Whatever he wants, he gets. Now, get the hell out of here, oh, and call your sister and tell her to come a few minutes early." Dad's paperwork lay in his lap untouched.

"If you don't fill that out, it's going to take you longer, Dad." I stood, ready to bolt if he tried to start something. He glared at me, then smiled. It was scary, since he did it so rarely.

"Sorry I'm such a pain in the ass, but I really hate doctors. Thanks for being here. Now, get out." Dad picked up his pen and started filling out the forms. I stood stock still, my mouth hanging open. It was the nicest thing he'd said to me in years. "I said go." Dad mumbled, then elbowed me in the knee.

"Yes, sir."

"Honey, I have a meeting at the Garden Club, and then

I'm getting fitted for the gown I'm wearing to the charity ball. Gage will take you to your doctor's appointment." Mom said. As usual, she was the only person capable of getting Dad to act like a somewhat reasonable person, though this morning the old man was putting up resistance.

"What the hell, Mary? I'm capable of driving myself. He needs to be closing the Granger deal." Dad glared at me. The breakfast room was painted bright yellow with red trim that Mom said was supposed to make everyone more cheerful in the morning. Feng shui? Whatever it was, its mystical powers were not working today.

"Frank, if I let you drive yourself you won't go. You'll end up at some greasy spoon and make your ulcer worse." She glanced at her watch impatiently, then noticed Dad's scowl. "This is not a request. Gage will take you to the appointment, but Trish will pick you up. She wants to take you to lunch. Now put your jacket on and scoot." She pecked him on the cheek, grabbed her purse and hurried out.

Mom refused to call my sister Trish by her nickname, Inky, and blissfully ignored the head to toe tattoos covering her. Living in a world of her own, my mother ignored what she didn't like and pretended that our family was perfect, as if we lived in a TV sitcom from the 1950s. I think that was why her marriage to Dad worked. She ignored his foul moods, and pretended he was the star of Leave it to Beaver.

"Good. She's gone. Now, this is what will really happen this morning."

"Shit." I groaned, then Dad carried on talking.

"You're going to take me to…" he grumbled, but was interrupted by Mom, who was standing at the door.

"Gage Scott Patterson, I'm going to wash your mouth out with soap! You know how much I hate the brown word.

Frank, if you bully Gage into letting you cancel that appointment, you will regret it. Trust me on this. Now, get in his truck and go. I have too much to do to be babysitting you today." She kissed Dad on the cheek again, then pecked mine for good measure. "Don't let him get away with his usual nonsense. Oh, and watch your language." She wagged her finger at me, then left.

"You heard her, Dad, let's get this over with." I sighed, not in the mood to deal with his tantrums today. Usually I'd let the verbal abuse slide, knowing when to pick my battles, but since my disastrous night with Lacey, I rivaled Dad for the title of Grumpiest Man in Raleigh.

"Fine, I'll go." Dad snatched his jacket off the back of his chair and stomped out. I took a few deep breaths and followed behind, hoping Dad would keep his mouth shut for the ride, but knowing he wouldn't.

"I know I keep harping on about this, but the Granger deal is very important to me and the firm. We stand to make a great deal of cash if we can get that hippy to sell those apartments." Dad uttered, then swiped at his forehead with the back of his hand. I noticed something I'd never seen before, or perhaps didn't want to notice. Fear. He was afraid, and maybe it was his mortality that had him on edge instead of his usual bad temper.

"Dad, I am heading over to the Millbrook Arms Apartments to speak with Mr. Parker. If he refuses to budge, I'll offer him an additional ten percent, as long as Mr. Granger approves it." I said. We were waiting for his appointment with the internist at UNC Rex Hospital.

"Don't worry about Donald Granger. He'll pony up any amount of money to buy that dump. Never forget that Donald has been a loyal client since I opened the business almost forty years ago. Whatever he wants, he gets. Now, get the hell out of here, oh, and call your sister and tell her to come a few minutes early." Dad's paperwork lay in his lap untouched.

"If you don't fill that out, it's going to take you longer, Dad." I stood, ready to bolt if he tried to start something. He glared at me, then smiled. It was scary, since he did it so rarely.

"Sorry I'm such a pain in the ass, but I really hate doctors. Thanks for being here. Now, get out." Dad picked up his pen and started filling out the forms. I stood stock still, my mouth hanging open. It was the nicest thing he'd said to me in years. "I said go." Dad mumbled, then elbowed me in the knee.

"Yes, sir."

Mom had asked me to take Dad to his appointment yesterday. Normally, I would have tried getting out of it, but I had an ulterior motive. The appointment was in an office building next to the hospital, and I wanted to speak with Lacey about the kiss.

I'd barely slept the night before, tossing and turning, my brain refusing to turn off. When I finally fell asleep, I relived that moment over and over in my dreams. Lacey had kissed me, and she was the one who started it. It was she who fell into my arms and temporarily made real what I'd dreamed about for years. What I didn't get was why she'd run away.

Seeking Lacey out at work was risky, and skirted the border of stalking, but I needed answers. Intruding on her life was not what I wanted to do, but I needed to know how she actually felt. Lacey would never have put her arms around me the way she did last night if the feeling was not mutual. That kiss felt real, and the way her body responded to mine felt real. But, if Lacey had decided she wanted nothing to do with me, I'd respect that. I might not like it, but I'd back off.

My pulse throbbed in my ear as I walked through the entrance of the ER. A small crowd was in the waiting area, so I stood behind them, hoping to pull myself together unobserved. I wasn't used to this feeling, the uneasiness of vulnerability I'd fought so hard to defeat since I'd left the Marines. Women flocked to me, chased me, and it was scary to find I was now doing the same to Lacey.

A male nurse with bright red hair I remembered from Dad's visit to the ER was working at the main desk. It took all of my self-control not to run out of the ER, to brave the few steps I had to walk to that desk. But, if I didn't force one foot in front of the other, I'd never know if I had a chance with Lacey or not. I took a deep breath and moved forward.

"Excuse me, you don't happen to know if Lacey Barnes is available?"

The nurse said nothing for a moment, looking me up and down with suspicion.

"Who wants to know?"

I thought people only said that in movies. My heart galloped in my chest, and I felt my throat closing up. Please, don't give me any problems, dude. I'm not here to hurt Lacey, only to get answers. I glanced at his name tag and addressed him properly.

"Powell, my name is Gage Patterson. Would you please tell her I am here, and that I'd like a word with her."

He pursed his lips and studied me for a few more uncomfortable seconds. Finally, he responded. "Just a moment, Sir. I'll see if she's able to speak with you." The man strolled away, turning his head around a couple of times, as if to make sure I wasn't following him. Jesus, did I look crazed or something?

After what seemed like forever, Lacey strolled into the reception area. Our eyes locked, and she stopped in her tracks. I could feel myself flushing and noticed a similar look on Lacey's face. She whispered something to the other nurse, laid a clipboard on the counter, and stepped forward.

"Let's go outside for a moment. I can't talk for long." Lacey muttered, then kept walking toward the entrance. I followed behind as casually as I could. Feeling like I was being watched, I turned my head back for a moment to see that nurse, Powell, observing us with narrowed eyes as we exited the building. Outside on the sidewalk, people milled around us, and I realized she'd done this for a reason, so we wouldn't be alone. She led me to a bus stop with a bench and we both sat, Lacey taking pains to keep a few inches of space between us. She looked over my shoulder, up to the overcast sky, anywhere but into my eyes. My hands itched to touch her, to pull her into my chest, and to kiss her with the passion I knew she felt too. A long moment passed, and at last the words I needed to say spilled out.

"Lacey, about the other night. I'm confused. You're the one who kissed me, and you have to understand I—"

"That was a mistake, Gage. It's my fault, and I assume full responsibility for it." Her emerald green eyes finally met mine, and they were glassy and wet. Lacey's discomfort was obvious, but she also needed to know my heart was breaking. I reached over, intending to take her hand, but she crossed her arms over her chest. My hand landed back in my lap with a thud.

"Lacey, I know you're feeling this too. The chemistry between us is real. I don't understand why you're denying it. Please, give me one more chance, give us one more chance. Let me take you to a movie, or a walk in the park. Let me just be with you." I pleaded in a whisper.

Lacey looked up to the sky, and her mouth angled down into a frown. Her hand reached toward mine, but she pulled it back, shook her head, and got to her feet.

"Look, Gage, it's just too soon. As you know I recently got dumped, left at the altar in front of hundreds of wedding guests. I only moved back to town two weeks ago, and dating is off the table. Being hurt again is something I'm not setting myself up for. If you'll excuse me, I need to get back to work. I'm very sorry, but I just can't do this right now." Lacey walked away. I stared after her, hoping she'd look back, but she never did.

At a stoplight on Capitol Boulevard I punched the steering wheel.

"Damn it, Lacey, why are you doing this?" I yelled, provoking a look from the driver beside me. I rolled up the window, sank in my seat and stared straight ahead. When the light turned green, I hit the gas and raced forward to get away from the pack of cars around me.

"I'm done. No more love. I've had a good life avoiding it. Drama is kept to a minimum, and I'm able to focus on my work and make great money. Commitment is for mental patients, not for me." My words were hollow though, and I knew it.

Moments later the Millbrook Arms Apartments came into view, and I turned into the pothole-ridden parking lot. Glancing around at the buildings, I wondered why Mr. Parker was resisting our offer. They were barely up to code, and couldn't be making him much money. The offer Donald Granger was making would set Parker up for the rest of his life. The North Raleigh area was being rebuilt with trendy shops and restaurants. Underneath the decrepit apartment buildings was land worth far more than he paid for.

"Mr. Parker, please let Granger write you a check, because I don't want to deal with my Dad kicking my ass if you don't." I muttered to myself, then picked up the folder on the passenger seat.

Dread filled me as I hopped out of the truck and headed toward the rental office. Nothing was going my way today, and I had a feeling this meeting wouldn't end with Parker signing a contract.

Inside the folder was an offer ten per cent higher than the last one. I was only allowed to show it to him if he balked at the original price again. I rang the bell, and after a few moments the door opened. Parker glared at me and started to shut it.

"Please, Mr. Parker. I need to speak with you." Good God, it was like every person I'd seen today was determined to give me a rough time.

"Mr. Patterson. I'm sorry, it's just you know what my answer will be." He waited for me to speak, and when I said nothing, he continued. "It's still no. I wish you'd stop bothering me with these offers, because it's useless." He said, then with a shake of his head he stepped aside, and ushered me into his office.

Parker was a throwback to the seventies, and peace signs and dust ruled his domain. He was solidly built, and his graying hair fell past his shoulders. A poster of John Lennon hung on the wall behind his desk, and I swore I could smell weed. He gestured toward the chair in front of his desk. After I sat, I leaned forward and placed the folder in front of him. He opened, then shut it with a look of disgust. Fuck me, what a waste of time.

"I've been authorized by Donald Granger to make you a new offer. It's ten per cent higher than the previous one." I muttered, my usual determination gone. All I could see in my mind was Lacey's face telling me to give up, to leave her alone. I had no energy left to talk this man into giving me a bong hit, much less selling us his property. Glancing out the side window, I saw a playground with kids playing on it, their mothers sitting on a dilapidated bench watching them. The swings and sliding board were old, built on a concrete slab. Half of the swings were missing seats, and weeds sprouted through cracks in the pavement. Why he wanted to hold on to this eyesore was beyond me.

"Do you want to know why I'm turning this down?" Parker's thin voice cut through the air. I turned back to him and nodded. He pushed the folder to my side of the desk.

"I bought this complex when the neighborhood hit bottom, when gunshots and sirens were heard on a daily basis. It cost next to nothing, and this current offer you're making..." He pointed at the folder, "...is almost twenty times what I paid for it. You probably think I'm a fool for turning you down."

"It has crossed my mind, sir." I murmured, shrugging my shoulders.

"Just now I saw you looking at those kids outside on the playground. Their parents struggle to find affordable housing, especially now that developers like yourself are pricing them out of the neighborhoods they've spent their entire lives in. Where are those kids to go? What about the real people who can't afford to pay the astronomical rents you want to charge them?" His thin lips pressed together, expecting me to put up an argument. I had none to give.

"I'm sorry to have bothered you Mr. Parker. Have a good day."

I had no fight left in me, so I gave him a half-smile, picked up the folder and strolled back to my truck. Before I hopped in the front seat I looked around, the peeling paint and drooping clotheslines next to the buildings standing in stark contrast to the new loft apartments sprouting up all over the neighborhood. But I could hear the sounds of happy children coming from the playground on the other side of the building. The argument Parker made was compelling, and I actually admired him for sticking to his guns.

Dad would make my life miserable, but I'd recommend to Mr. Granger that he look for another property. There were other rundown buildings in the area he could bulldoze. Hopefully he'd leave Mr. Parker and the residents who lived here in peace.

Chapter Seven

LACEY

"Are you the new tenant? I saw movers bringing stuff in this morning, and I've never seen you around before. Oh, my name is Inky." A beautiful woman with dark hair covered in tattoos held her hand out for me to shake. I put my basket of laundry down and took her hand in mine.

"It's a pleasure to meet you. My name is Lacey, and yes, I'm the new tenant." The woman was friendly, which added to my good feelings about the move. I loved my new apartment, and if I could make a friend or two in the building, so much the better.

"Moving is a pain in the ass. Are you new to the area?" She tossed detergent in the washer and stuffed her clothes inside.

"Yes, and no. I'm from here, but I've been gone for about ten years now. Just moved back. Raleigh has changed an awful lot since I've been gone. You don't happen to know of a place to find antiques, or vintage furniture? I only brought my bedroom with me, and I don't want the usual boring stuff you find at chain furniture stores." It broke my heart to give up so much of my furniture in the move, but I was determined to start over from scratch. A fresh start in every way, not just where I lived.

"I like you more just hearing that. No boring furniture, or anything at all for that matter. Yes, I know a lot of places to discover cool stuff. Maybe we can go shopping together. Actually, I have a better idea," She leaned over and turned the washer on.

"Put your clothes in the washer and you can come up to my place. We can have a glass of wine, and I can show off my furniture. I'd like to think I have funky taste. Oh, and I'll give you the lay of the land, tell you which of our neighbors to avoid, that sort of thing." Her smile was infectious, and I grinned in response. What the hell, it could be fun. I could also use a new friend.

***

"This is home. Sorry it's a mess, but I'm allergic to cleaning. Well, except for the kitchen and bathroom. I'm not completely gross." My new neighbor let us into her apartment, and I was in love with the way she'd decorated. It suited her to a T. Unique artwork hung on the walls, brightly colored paintings that matched the tattoos covering her skin. She was right about the clutter. There was barely an empty spot on the tables, most of them filled with miniature Asian sculptures and bonsai plants. What struck me was how homey it felt, very comfortable and lived in.

"Have a seat and I'll pour us a glass. Merlot okay?" She asked. I nodded and sat on a dusky purple velvet couch. Moments later she sat next to me and lifted her glass.

"A toast; to new neighbors and friends." Her smile was so huge and warm, and oddly familiar. I wondered for a moment if we'd met before, maybe as children?

"Okay, now let's talk about the lay of the land. Most of the peeps living here have been around a long time. They're a friendly bunch, and we have little get-togethers regularly. There are a couple of them you need to watch out for. On the first floor next to the entrance is an elderly man, Mr. Greenly. He's grumpy, but harmless. We all keep an eye out for him since he lives alone. Which apartment did you get?" Her words came out in a gush, and it took a moment for me to remember my unit number.

"I'm on the sixth floor, 603."

"You took Grace's old place. I'm proud to say my match-making abilities hit solid gold with her. I introduced her to her husband, Merrick. So you have me to thank for your new apartment." She sipped her wine, then put her index finger on her chin, and asked the question I dreaded most.

"Are you single? Or seeing someone special?" She cocked her head to the side and waited for my answer.

"Yes, and no. But, I'm recently out of a relationship, so I'm kinda keeping to myself if you know what I mean." I took a big gulp of my wine, hoping my answer would keep her from wanting to set me up with somebody. Plus, and I knew it was crazy, but I was hoping to hear from Gage. I'd told him to leave me alone, but a small part of me regretted that decision. Sleepless nights had been filled with images of him, and every time my phone buzzed, I'd hold my breath hoping he'd contacted me, despite me telling him not to.

"That's too bad, because there's a bartender at work who is relentlessly single, hot, and I'd love to see him with someone steady. His name is Mark. Oh, you must come to my bar. It's called Inky's, and it's only a few blocks away. Your first drink will be my treat!" She said.

"I will, as long as you don't try to set me up with Mark." I laughed. She faked a frown and then giggled.

"Sorry, I can't help it. I feel like the world is a gray place, so I'm always setting up my friends, adding color to their lives, know what I mean?" She said, then continued the interrogation. "So where did you move here from?" She asked. I could tell it would be easy to open up to her, but I didn't want to give her my life story yet.

"Boston. I got a job at UNC Rex Hospital and decided to make a fresh start here in my hometown. It's been great being back, for the most part. Actually, I had an ex-boyfriend hit me up already." I said, then mentally kicked myself for saying too much. Her face lit up.

"Really? That's fast. Are you going to go out with him?" She stood up and darted to the kitchen without waiting for my reply. When she returned, she had the wine bottle with her. She poured herself another glass and topped mine off. I mulled my words over, then gave in to the need to tell someone about how I really felt.

"Let's just say it's the wrong time. I'm still attracted to him, and the chemistry is like, wow, off the charts. But I need to spend some time on my own. All I'm interested in now is settling in and finding my groove here. If it was just a simple fling, or a friends with benefits situation, I'd be all for it. There's just too much history between us though, so I don't see it being simple, or a fling. He wants more, and I'm not in the right headspace for anything serious." I said, formulating in words what I'd been thinking since I'd told Gage I didn't want to see him anymore. "I can tell you're a bartender, because I'm telling you stuff I've not even said aloud to myself." I raised my glass to her, and she laughed. Then her eyes widened, and she grabbed my hand.

"Hey, I've got a fabulous idea. You wanna play dress up and crash a party? And when I say dress up, I mean wear something special, like an evening gown. It's this Saturday, and it's probably going to be a little boring, but the food will be excellent, and it's free booze. You can be my plus one! Please? I don't want to go alone. My brother is throwing it, mostly to impress his clients. I'll wear this cool flapper dress I got at a vintage clothing shop a couple of blocks from here. Let me show it to you." She raced to her bedroom and returned with a stunning vintage beaded dress, bright red, my favorite color. I thought about it for less than a second.

"Yes, I would love to go to this party with you."

* * *

Work kept me busy all week, which helped since it bummed me out that Gage never texted or called. I guessed my words got through to him, and he would respect my wishes after all. I told him it was bad timing, that I didn't want us to rekindle what was a teenage romance, but… damn, I still kind of hoped he'd try. In theory, I was relieved. Realistically, part of me regretted telling him to back off. Whatever, I was the one who decided not to pursue it. My heart was still healing from my last relationship, and I didn't need the pressure of a new one. Life was too short for regrets, and I didn't need a man to make me feel complete.

Seven o'clock rolled around, and I had promised Inky I'd meet her at eight. Time to pull out the fancy gown I kept in the back of the closet wrapped in plastic. It was what I was supposed to have worn to my wedding reception on the beach, and I'd spent a small fortune on it. I'd sold my wedding dress immediately after the botched wedding, but always felt that one day I'd get some use out of this gown.

When I pulled it out, I felt my throat closing up and pressure building behind my eyes. I knew I hadn't been in love with Joseph, but that didn't mean the pain wasn't real. As I pulled the delicate fabric out of the wardrobe bag, a wave of despair rolled through me. Sitting on the side of the bed, I held the gown to my chest and struggled not to cry. I realized I was crushing it, so I laid it next to me, then fell back on the mattress and curled up on my side.

"What if it had been someone I really cared for who stood me up? I wasn't even in love with Joseph and I'm still in mourning for our relationship. What if it had been Gage who abandoned me at the altar?" I whispered. A tear dropped from my cheek to the mattress. I stood up and headed to the bathroom to splash cold water on my face.

"Stop caring about this. It was for the best. Joseph not showing up proves how little you can trust men. He didn't care about me enough to tell me he didn't want to go through with the marriage, humiliating me in front of everyone we knew. If we hadn't worked at the same hospital, I'd probably still be in Boston, happily getting on with my life." I stated to my reflection in the mirror. "Just stop caring and give yourself a little TLC for a change."

Of course, the bitch of the matter was, I did care about love. If I didn't care, I wouldn't have given Gage a second thought, and I wouldn't be so torn up inside at the thought of never hearing from him again. How could I not care for him? The night we parted was burned in my memory, and the attraction hadn't gone away. If anything it had grown. When I went to Harvard, and even beyond school, I went on a string of first dates, always turning the second date down, because they just couldn't compare to him. But did I want to set myself up for rejection again? I answered aloud, to the judgemental eyes gazing at me from the mirror.

"Hell no. Who needs a man anyway? Now let's put on some makeup and have a good time. Inky's your date for the evening, and we will have a blast."

"Wow, you look stunning." Inky surprised me with a hug, then stood back from her door. "What do you think?" She asked, then spun around. Her raven-black hair had been meticulously finger waved and lacquered to a high shine. The bright colors of her tattoos glowed with a sheen, and I could detect a hint of golden powder accentuating her shoulders and chest.

"You look drop-dead gorgeous. Seriously, I'm not just saying that. Oh, and that beaded bag matches your dress perfectly." I stood back and admired her.

"Well, I do have a confession to make. We might be a little overdressed, but my brother's work parties can sometimes be a little dull. I want to liven it up a bit. You'll like him, he's also single and very handsome, or at least that's what all the girls say." She winked, then turned and shut her door.

"You know my answer to that. No men." I laughed. She grabbed my hand and dragged me to the elevator. When we got in, she surprised me.

"Why are you hitting the button for the penthouse? I thought we were going out?" I asked as the elevator doors closed behind us.

"My brother lives there. The reason I go to his boring parties is I can drink and have fun, and not have to worry about driving home. Feel free to imbibe as much booze as you can safely hold, and eat all you want. Getting home is a breeze, and you won't break any laws either."

Moments later the elevator opened. She took my hand and led me to the solitary door in the tiny hallway.

"It's probably not as boring as I let on. He always invites potential clients though, and warns me to be on my best behavior. I'm usually good for the first half of the evening. For the second half, anything goes." She winked and opened the door.

Bossa Nova music filled the space, and several couples were already on the improvised dance floor, which I assumed was the living room, but most of the furniture was gone. Our host also had a substantial art collection, but his was more elegant and refined than his sister's. Subdued paintings filled the walls, which were painted a muted heather with soft track lighting giving the room a subtle glow. Her brother had great taste, and I could see why the room was already full, despite it being relatively early.

"You were right, we are a tad overdressed." I murmured, and Inky cackled.

"All eyes will be on us, and we'll be the hit of the party. I hope you can dance. My parents are very conservative, sent me to finishing school to learn how to dance and be a proper lady. I might not be a lady, but I am the queen of the tango, so I expect you to dance your ass off." She grabbed two glasses of champagne off a waiter's tray, and handed me one.

The champagne was superb, which surprised me. Most functions like this served the cheap stuff. I snuck a glance at Inky, envious of her perpetual smile. It had been so long since I'd cut loose and had fun. Tonight I would forget about my problems and really live, have a good time. Instead of taking another small sip of the bubbly, I downed my glass.

"Atta girl!" Inky smacked me on the shoulder. "I like your style, Lacey. But before we get carried away, let's grab some hors d'oeuvres. Don't want to get too drunk, too fast." She looped her arm through mine and dragged me to a table laden with goodies. Inky picked up two small plates and handed me one, and then I heard a deep, gravelly voice speak from behind us.

"Inky. You look ravishing as usual. Who are you with?"

I put my plate down because my hands were trembling, the nerve endings in my skin coming alive at the sound of him. I turned slowly around and confronted the devilish man that had haunted my thoughts since I'd run away from him. A rakish grin spread across his face when our eyes met.

"Hello, Gage."

Chapter Eight

GAGE

"So, you've met my sister, Inky?"

It stunned me to see Lacey with her. Knowing she was downstairs on the sixth floor was challenging, and I debated nightly if I should knock on her door or not. So far, I'd stood in front of it twice, wondering how Lacey would react if she opened the door to see me with a smile and a boner. Common sense had prevailed.

Knowing my bed was above hers, and that I could be on her doorstep in less than two minutes, made every second I spent alone even more torturous. Looking at her now, it took every ounce of self-control not to kick everyone out and drag her to my bedroom.

Lacey was downright elegant, like she was attending a high-society function. Her normally wavy strawberry-blonde hair was straightened and hanging past her bare, milky white shoulders. Her scarlet gown clung to her curves, and the only jewelry she wore was a simple gold chain with a solitary emerald hanging between her ample cleavage.

Everyone in the room had noticed Lacey and Inky's

entrance. My eyes traveled up her body, inch by inch until our eyes met. Lacey's wide-eyed look of wonder confirmed my suspicions. She didn't know Inky was my sister. I might not be superstitious, or really religious, but I was starting to believe in fate. How else could she be here?

Lacey turned to Inky and stared hard at her, then swiveled in my direction.

"Now it makes sense why you looked familiar." Lacey avoided my eyes. "She and I met in the laundry room and hit it off. You know, I'd wondered if we'd met as kids or something, though I'm bewildered that we've not run into each other before." Lacey said, then took a healthy gulp of her cocktail.

"You two know each other? It's a small world, isn't it?" My sister said, then got a look in her eye that terrified me.

"Inky, we went to high school together. I've told you about her before. Lacey Barnes? We were, um, very close in our senior year. Remember?" I said, winking.

I didn't want to put Lacey on the spot by going into the details of our prior relationship. She'd already made it clear she wanted nothing from me, and even though my cock was half hard just being in the same room with her, I'd do my best to respect that. If she only wanted a casual friendship, so be it. Lacey would be mine again, but she would come to me when she was good and ready.

"You're Lacey? How the hell didn't I… well, it's nice to meet you after all these years. I heard an awful lot about you." Inky's grin grew wider, and I could see the wheels spinning in her head. I would have to take her aside and tell her to lay off the matchmaking. She'd never tried it before with me, because she knew I wasn't into relationships. Now she could see an opening, a way to work her meddlesome magic.

"If you guys are brother and sister, how come we never met? I used to spend a lot of time with Gage when we were teenagers." Lacey wondered. Inky placed her drink on a table and took a step back.

"Mom shipped me off to fancy-ass Saint Margaret's Finishing School in Virginia to make a lady out of me. It's a stuffy girls boarding academy, and I'm still recovering from the scars it left on my soul. As you can see..." Inky spun around and threw her arms in the air, "...it utterly failed!"

The three of us burst into laughter, and I was so grateful for my sister's ability to put anyone at ease. When I'd first noticed the two of them walk through the door, my heart had skipped a beat, and I deliberately held back, waiting for them to get drinks before coming forward. I didn't want to look too anxious, or desperate. Though, the way my heart was beating now, I wondered if that was how bad it had gotten. Shit, desperation wasn't a good look on anyone.

"So how did you get the penthouse? I mean, I know your Dad's real-estate firm owns the place, but I had no idea you lived here. Why didn't you tell me you lived in this building?" A suspicious look settled on Lacey's face, replacing the easy grin from just a moment ago. Shit, she was going there.

"Dad doesn't own this building. Gage does." Inky said, then snatched Lacey's empty glass from her hand, and strolled to the bar to get refill it. Lacey crossed her arms over her chest, eyes narrowed.

"When I signed the lease, it said Patterson Realty." Lacey stated.

"And that's the name of my company," I drawled. "Dad's business is Raleigh Real Estate & Development. We share an office, you know, work together, though he forgets that most of the time." I sighed, seeing this battle was probably lost, and yet another load of bullshit would come between us. She'd think horrible things about me, and I'd have to change her mind. Again.

Lacey glanced away, a shadow passing over her face. When she looked back, my shoulders stiffened, knowing whatever she had to say would not be good.

"Wait, a minute. The rent you're charging is half of what I paid in Boston. I realize this is a smaller city, but it makes little sense that I got such a good deal. You aren't expecting some kind of quid pro quo arrangement? Expecting me to sleep with you in exchange for paying lower rent? Because if you are you'll be…"

"Here you go, Lacey." Inky handed her a drink. "Oh look, some of my employees are here. Since you're new in town, they'll be excellent friends to have. Let me introduce you." She looped her arm through Lacey's, but she shrugged it off.

"Inky, if you don't mind, I need to have a word with Gage. Alone." She glared at me. Inky gave me the side eye, then her. "Yeah… I'll talk to you both in a little while." She hightailed it to the other side of the room, a look of confusion on her face.

Fuck me, she was going to let me have it. The question was, did I want it to be in public, or could I drag her somewhere in private, so she wouldn't give me grief in front of my guests. My eyes darted around the room, then I saw that the balcony was empty.

"Lacey, let's take this outside." I grasped her elbow, intending to lead her forward, but she shook it off. Lacey stretched her arm out, indicating I should go first and she'd follow.

Fine. Be that way.

The balcony stretched the length of the building, so I took her to the furthest corner away from the sliding glass doors. My heart galloped in my chest, afraid she was going to either cuss me out or slug me. If this was anybody else, I would've laughed it off and sent them packing. This was Lacey, and I could see why she might think I was doing something shady. Thing was, I wasn't. Maybe I could change the subject? Get her to focus on something else, anything but me and what she was accusing me of.

I leaned against the railing and glanced up. There was a full moon, and even the stars looked brighter than usual. I turned to see Lacey's face in her hands, and she was shaking her head. Without thinking, I put my arm around her and drew her closer. Removing her hands from her face, she glared in my direction.

"Gage, please say you're charging me the same rent as everyone else. Please, tell me this entire arrangement, me signing that lease wasn't a way to get me in your bed. I remember that woman from the restaurant, angry that you couldn't even remember her name. I'm not lining up to be another one of your conquests."

I pressed my lips together, not used to being questioned about my ethics. Honestly, it was pissing me off.

"Lacey, you are paying the same rent as everyone else. Go ask anyone in there, well, except my sister. She gets the family discount." I bit my tongue, not wanting to say anything to make things worse.

"Yeah, right? You will not expect any type of special 'compensation' from me? Because if you are, you can forget about it." Lacey bit her words off and started to stalk off. I grabbed her shoulder and spun her around.

"What the hell? Why do you think I'd pull one over on

you? I don't need to pull tricks to get any woman in bed, and the fact you think I would speaks volumes for how you really feel about me. Shit, that woman at Beasley's restaurant? Damn right, I didn't remember her name. You know why? Because I didn't give two shits about her." I ran my fingers through my hair, realizing how callous that made me sound. "That woman knew all along that I wanted nothing serious. I made it perfectly clear from the very start."

Lacey played her hands on her hips and glared at me with her brilliant green eyes.

"I care about you, not some silly girl who apparently couldn't understand that I wanted nothing more than a one-night stand." I took a deep breath, trying to keep my temper in check. "You know, maybe you're right. This isn't the time for us. Maybe it's just some fucked-up fantasy in my head that you and I could still have something, that our connection never went away."

No one, not even Lacey Barnes would get away with accusing me of this underhanded shit. "Now if you'll excuse me, I have guests to attend to. Enjoy the party."

"I don't know what went down with you two, but Lacey looks miserable. I tried to get her to talk, but she clams up and says nothing's wrong." Inky whispered in my ear. I glanced over at her standing in a corner nursing her drink. I'd kept my eyes on her all night, noticing that wherever I went, she was always a few feet away. Not talking, just staring at me as I talked to clients and friends.

"Lacey had the nerve to accuse me of giving her cheap rent so I could get in her pants. You know me, Inky. I don't have to resort to stupid tactics like that to get anyone in bed." I turned away from Lacey, hoping she didn't see the anger boiling inside me.

"Shit. Do you want me to say something to her?" Inky asked, then glanced in her direction. Lacey looked away, and I knew she could see we were talking about her. I was about to beg my sister not to say anything, when Lacey pushed herself off the wall and sauntered over.

"Can I have a word with you Gage?" She said, and I noticed her words were slurred, just the tiniest bit. I glanced down at her hand, noticing she'd switched from champagne to something more potent. Her green eyes were wet, and I felt my knees growing weak. I couldn't resist her, never could. Lacey could ask me for anything and I'd give it to her.

"Excuse us." I nodded to Inky, took Lacey's elbow and led her back to the balcony. Another couple was in our old spot, so I walked us to the other side which faced the busy streets of downtown.

Lacey leaned against the railing. I joined her, careful to stand a few inches away. She was staring at the traffic down below, then she turned and faced me, her skin paler than usual.

"I'm sorry. I shouldn't have accused you of what I did. I, well, I was being a brat. You didn't deserve it." Lacey murmured, looking down at her feet. I reached out and placed my hand on her shoulder, rewarded by a small smile crossing her face as she stared into my eyes.

"Apology accepted. Though, for the record I'll never, ever resort to dirty tricks like that. If you want to be left alone, I'll respect your wishes." I wanted to pull her into my arms, touch her, feel her warmth underneath the palms of my hands, but I resisted the urge. No way was I going to scare her off now. Lacey turned back toward the railing, then looked up.

"Do you see the stars above us? They're beautiful." When she pointed up a cloud passed over. "Damn it, the moon is gone now." Her voice trailed off, and she moved an inch closer. My arm itched to wrap around her, to pull Lacey tight against me. I wanted to touch her so damn bad. Instead, I hoped my words could bring her to me, willingly, not coerced.

"Look down at the street, at the cars below us. All the flashing, sparkling lights you'd ever want. I often stand out here alone to think, you know, to clear my head. Something about the stars overhead and the cars driving below makes me feel like nothing can touch me. Like nothing can touch us." I whispered. Lacey's smile widened, then she looked down like it embarrassed her. Fuck me, she didn't need to feel ashamed of anything around me. It was as if she was afraid of her feelings, afraid, shit, that I'd hurt her.

How could I breach this wall she'd erected between us?

"Just because you aren't pulling something shady on me to get in my pants, it doesn't mean you will have your way with me. I know you Gage Patterson. In high school you had everyone wrapped around your finger, always getting anything you wanted." Lacey said, biting her lower lip. Damn, I wanted to do that for her, nibble on her full red lips, then cover her mouth with mine. But first, I had to make her want it. I took Lacey's hand and pulled her inside.

"Where are you taking me?" She asked as I led her through the sea of couples dancing. I turned and stood before her. We stared into each other's eyes for what seemed like forever, and then I crushed her into my chest.

"Let's dance, baby." I smiled, though I knew she would push back. Call it intuition, but I sensed her need, her desire to be touched. She pressed her chest against mine, and I could feel her heartbeat hammering inside of her.

"You are the most beautiful woman in this room." I whispered, then gently kissed the tender flesh beneath her ear. She fell slightly forward and wrapped her arms tightly around my waist. A soft moan escaped from her throat.

Mission accomplished.

"You are such a neanderthal, thinking you can do whatever you want. Jesus, Gage, what's gotten into you?" Lacey said, but the entire time she was bitching, she was also melting into my arms, moving her feet in response to mine, rubbing her body against me. I placed my index finger under her chin, and lifted it so her lips were inches away.

"You've always been such a romantic." Lacey whispered. I chuckled, knowing she was the only person ever to accuse me of that.

"Lacey," My lips glanced off the side of her neck, and then I whispered in her ear, "You are the one woman in my life who's ever said that, much less thought it. You know why?" I asked. She shook her head, locking those intense emerald green eyes to mine. "Because you're the reason. I've only ever been romantic with you."

A fight broke out between two tenants who lived next to each other, both complaining about the other being noisy. Putting them in the same room with booze had not been the brightest idea I'd ever had, so I left Lacey to break it up. When I returned, she was chatting with Inky, and the crowd was thinning out. I was about to cut in when I felt a tap on my shoulder.

"Have you seen our host, Gage Patterson?" Cameron, my former tenant asked me, a curious look on his face.

Smart ass.

"Fuck you, Cam. What are you talking about?" I blushed, knowing exactly what he was talking about.

"Well, my friend Gage doesn't believe in relationships, only in casual sex. No commitments for him, no siree. Doesn't want to be tied down, a no-strings-attached kind of guy. I was talking to his sister who tells me that he is mooning over someone." He scanned the crowd, then pointed toward Lacey. "That girl. The one I saw you with at Beasley's restaurant. She's the one making Gage insane."

"I don't want to talk about it."

Cam said nothing. He didn't have to. The shit-eating grin on his face forced me to respond.

"Fine. Just don't spread it around. I got a reputation, know what I mean?" I shrugged my shoulders, then poked him in the chest. "You promise not to run around town with this?" I asked. Cam rolled his eyes, then nodded. I gave him the quick version of my relationship with Lacey.

"So, you're telling me that this is your high-school sweetheart you've never gotten over? Like for ten years? Damn, you've got it bad." Cam laughed, and I felt a flush creeping up my face.

"Who the hell are you to talk? You and Marcy are…" I began, then a couple of guests interrupted us to say their goodbyes. Marcy sidled up to me while I was giving them my thanks for coming and sang in my ear.

"Lacey and Gage sitting in a tree…"

"Fuck. You. Marcy." I said as the couple took off. She jumped away, afraid I really meant it. I opened my arms.

"Come to Papa Bear, Marcy." I laughed. She wrapped

her arms around my waist and kissed me on the cheek. Then she let go of me and threw her arms around her husband.

"We'd better go before the big bad bear gets mad." She said to Cam, who threw up his hands in mock fear.

"Too late." Cam glanced at his watch. "Yeah, looks like the party's winding down. I need to make sure the sitter gets home in time. Let's get together soon, you know, the four of us." He winked.

"Get out, both of you!" I laughed, then hustled them to the door. Shit, I didn't want my friends speculating about something I was unsure of. Lacey might be responding to me now, but that could change on a dime. Moments later, all thoughts of Lacey turning me away flew out the window, as she stumbled over to me and whispered in my ear.

"Do you want me to stay with you tonight?"

Chapter Nine

GAGE

"Your party was fabulous, though I must admit I think it was the company. Usually they're a big snooze fest." Inky teased, swaying just the teensiest bit on her heels.

Only the three of us remained; her, me, and Lacey. We were on the balcony, enjoying the nighttime sky and the chill breeze coming in off the river. I was torn between telling Inky to hightail it out of there, and keeping her as a buffer between Lacey and me. Tension had been building since she asked to stay the night. If I was smart, I'd get my sister to take Lacey home. But I'd never been smart when it came to this woman. Moments later, my dilemma was solved when Inky did something, well, Inky-like.

"I need to go to the powder room." She abruptly announced and walked inside. Seconds later I heard the heavy thud of a door slamming, then silence. For a couple of minutes we stood there leaning against the railing, not speaking. With anyone else it would have been uncomfortable, and I'd be wracking my brain for words to fill the silence, but not with Lacey. My eyes darted between her oval, pale face and her hand resting less than an inch from mine. I itched to hold it.

Jesus Christ, was I afraid? Was that what this was about? Why on earth was I afraid of Lacey? I'd never been afraid of a woman before in my life, but she terrified me. Of all the women I'd known, and I couldn't remember the names of most, Lacey was the only one who made me sweat. She was such a lady, and always carried herself with a dignity I only dreamed of possessing. Maybe she was out of my league, and that was why… no, she'd definitely been turned on tonight. Hell, she asked to stay the night. Stop doubting yourself.

"Your sister's not coming back, is she?" Lacey murmured, then turned slightly in my direction. Her warm breath against my neck had my cock at full mast, and it took all of my willpower not to turn and grind it into her. She'd kept me turned on all night rubbing up against me. When we danced I nearly came in my pants, her breasts pressed so tight against my body. I had to remind myself not to let my hands slide down and cup her round ass, knowing if I did I might scare her off. When we were dancing, I felt her erect nipples through the thin fabric of her gown. I wanted to touch them, feel them, and taste those pink nubs.

"I'd guess not." I said, realizing that Inky had pulled the rabbit out of her hat, the matchmaking magic in full strength, leaving us alone to work out this thing between us, though I hoped it was Lacey throwing herself into my arms. But, there was one little problem.

Lacey was drunk.

Lacey swiped her forehead with the back of her hand, her mouth half open and eyes wide and glassy. If this was anyone else, I'd be dragging them to the bedroom. But, not Lacey. She'd had too much to drink, and as much as I wanted her, there was no way I'd take advantage of her in this state. I was completely screwed when it came to taking things slow with this woman. What I needed to do was get Lacey back to the safety of her own bed, saving her from my desire to lean her over the railing, lift her dress up and fuck her while she screamed my name over and over again.

"What are you thinking? You look so intense." Lacey whispered, then grabbed me by the waist and pulled me into her. Her foot stepped on mine and she stumbled, then crashed into me. Lacey shook her head back and forth and giggled.

"You okay, baby?" I asked, then placed my hands on her cheeks and gazed deep into her soulful green eyes, stroking her soft cheek. I pulled her into my chest, and whispered into her ear, "I'm going to take you back to your place."

Lacey laughed and pulled away, grabbing my hands at the same time. "I know you don't want to do that, Gage Patterson. C'mon, give me the tour of your penthouse. All I've seen is the balcony, the bathroom, and your living room."

I bit my lip to keep from laughing. How our roles had reversed. The way Lacey was looking at me, she wanted more than just the grand tour. All I could think about was how to get her back to her own apartment, safe from my greedy mouth and cock.

"Are you sure you don't want me to walk you home? I think you've had too much to drink, and…"

Lacey laughed, then pulled me toward the sliding doors. As we stepped inside, she tripped and threw an arm around my shoulder to right herself.

"Oops." Lacey giggled, then she kicked off her heels. I should've persuaded her to step away from the bar a little earlier in the evening. What was left of the booze was on the far side of the living room, so I led her in the opposite direction toward the bedrooms. I had no intention of letting her into mine. That would be pushing my self-control to its limits. Instead, I hoped to steer Lacey toward one of the guest rooms.

"I want to see your bed." She giggled, then she fell against the wall outside my bedroom door. How she guessed it was mine was beyond me, but that was where she fell. Her laughter stopped, and she held her stomach.

"I don't feel so good." Lacey slurred, then glanced away, her face flushing.

Shit!

"C'mon Lacey, hold it in for just a minute, okay." I muttered, wanting to get her to the closest bathroom, which of course was in my bedroom. When I opened the door, Lacey practically fell through it, and then to my surprise she climbed onto my bed, laughing and patting the mattress beside her.

"Gage, come here." Lacey said in a sing-song voice, then she burst into laughter. All evidence of her feeling sick had disappeared, and I wondered if it hadn't been a ruse just to climb into my bed.

"Are you sure you feel alright, because you looked awful just a minute ago, babe." I stood in front of her with my hands on my hips, wanting to both take her in my arms and spank her, and not in the warm and friendly way.

"Don't tell me you've forgotten how to have sex in the last ten years?" Lacey asked, then stretched out on the bed while my hormones surged. How the hell was I supposed to do this? If she woke up tomorrow and wondered what the hell I was doing with her naked, she'd flip out. I could virtually guarantee it, especially if she didn't remember anything. No way was I giving in to this temptation, not if she wasn't sober.

"Lacey, trust me, I've not forgotten how to make you hot. But that's not the issue here. You've had too much to drink. Also, the first time I make love with you after all these years, I want you to remember it." While I talked she stood up, lifted her dress over her head, where it got stuck for a moment before she finally got it off, then she threw it across the room.

"Oh my God." I muttered, shaking my head.

Then, she reached behind her, and struggled to unhook her sheer black bra.

"Lacey, what are you doing? Babe, seriously, you are a sight for sore eyes, and I've wished for this moment ever since you came back into my life, but I'm not going to fuck it up doing something stupid like this."

She abandoned her bra and reached for her black lace panties, but then she fell back on the bed. Seeing her smooth skin presented to me like that made my brain momentarily shut off. I sat down next to her prone form and smoothed my hand over her taut stomach.

"Gage, I know you want me. I want you too. Now. Hell, if you won't go all the way, how about a little kiss, you know, for old times' sake?" Lacey propped herself up on her elbows and her green eyes swept over my body, starting at my face and slowly moving south until they landed on my crotch. Her eyes clouded over, then she reached behind her again and the bra finally came loose.

Jesus, this woman was trying to kill me. Her tits were the perfect size, not too big nor too small, and her hard little nipples beckoned to me. I wanted to lick them, kiss them while sliding my fingers into her hot, wet slit. Then, I'd slide down her body, rip her panties off, and taste her...

"Oh, fuck me." I sighed and swiped my mouth with the back of my hand. "Don't do it." My dick was so hard now it hurt, but there was no way I was touching her when she was in no condition to give me her consent.

"One kiss. That's it, Lacey Barnes, only one, and then I'm turning out this light and you are going to sleep here. I'm going to sleep in the guest room." My voice shook. Fuck, I shouldn't be doing this. I was risking a future with this woman for a simple kiss. But then again, nothing had ever been simple with Lacey. I climbed on top of her and cupped her face in my hands, stroking her pale cheeks and staring into those insane eyes that had haunted my dreams for years.

"What are you waiting for?" Lacey whispered. Her hand stretched out, grabbing the back of my neck, then she squeezed it while guiding my lips until they hovered over hers. Our eyes locked, and every memory I had of the two of us in my bed during our one steamy summer together flashed through my mind. Then my lips crashed into hers.

The taste of her mouth sent shock waves through me. It dissipated moments later as her tongue licked my closed lips, encouraging me to open to her. Lacey's tongue dipped inside, and a deep moan rumbled through her chest. The hand on my neck pulled me down further, deepening the kiss. My groans mixed with hers, our chests vibrating against each other as our mouths explored what they'd been missing for so long. Reverent and soft at first, restrained passion transformed into primal need when I felt her other hand grab my ass. Lacey's lips left mine and connected to the sensitive skin under my ear, and my groan became a full-on growl. My fingers found her now-tangled hair and pulled, then kneaded the thick blonde locks. Lacey's hips bucked, pressing her crotch against mine. Our bodies rocked together, and the friction of her pushing her pussy against my erection was threatening to make me into the animal I was trying to avoid becoming. Lacey's lips found mine again, and it felt like she wanted to swallow me whole. If this went on much longer I'd let her. Hell, I'd take her with the force I knew she craved.

God Almighty, where did she learn to kiss like this?

A little voice broke through in the back of my head, screaming for me to stop. I pulled back and her teeth took my bottom lip, gently tugging, wanting more. My heart felt like it would burst, and then, with lust still racing through my veins I rolled off of her and somehow ended up on the floor. I gasped for air, my body not quite ready to understand the common sense my brain was trying to hammer into it. Once I got my breathing under control, I picked myself up and stood over Lacey, who had the glazed look of a woman on the verge of either losing control or passing out. My inner voice echoed inside, urging me to leave now.

"I'm stepping out of the room for a few minutes." I muttered.

"Wait." Lacey pleaded, "I'm sorry."

"You did nothing wrong, Lacey, but if I don't leave now, I might do something we'll both regret."

"Gage, where have you been?" Lacey murmured as I shut the bedroom door behind me. I'd paced back and forth along the length of the balcony for the last ten minutes, bringing myself down from the dangerous high I'd felt minutes ago.

"Cooling off. How are you feeling?"

Lacey was under the blankets, her head propped up by

pillows. Her now bloodshot eyes were half shut, and she had a serene smile stretched across her face.

"I'm thinking about our first kiss." Lacey patted the bed. "Come here." Her words were slurring even more than before. Instead of the bed, I sat on the chaise lounge by the window.

"Gage, did I ever tell you that when we first met I couldn't take my eyes off you? I mean, that first day of school you were the only boy I saw, and that I thought about you all day long?" She whispered, then yawned.

"No, you never did. But it was the same for me, Lacey, and I've never forgotten a single minute we've spent together since." I stretched out on the chaise, my feet hanging off the end, and kicked my shoes off. I glanced over at her and saw her eyes closed, and wondered if she would remember anything about tonight. The dancing, the laughing, and the primal kiss that was like no other we'd shared before.

"I've missed you Lacey, so damn much." I whispered.

Her breathing slowed, and minutes later when I heard her softly snoring, I stood and gazed down at her, wondering how I'd ever survive if she didn't feel the same way I did.

This woman could destroy me. I'd never felt this way about anyone before, and if I was even remotely sane when it came to Lacey, I would leave her be, never bother her again. Protect my heart the way I always had, by ignoring it.

The urge to climb in bed and hold her tight was overwhelming. But, how would she react in the morning to find me there, spooning her?

Instead of giving in to temptation, I kissed her forehead.

"I'm going to make you mine, Lacey Barnes." I whispered, and reluctantly left to sleep alone in the guest room.

Chapter Ten

LACEY

Oh my God, I felt like shit.

The pounding in my skull was unbelievable, and every muscle in my body was screeching at me for drinking gin like it was Kool-aid. A pillow was over my face, and when I removed it, I noticed a damp spot on the sheet where I must have been drooling. The heavy black curtains were shut, except for an inch or two, and even that amount of light forced me to hide under the blankets to block it out. Wait, a minute. The drapes I'd ordered for my bedroom hadn't arrived yet. Plus, they were yellow.

This wasn't my apartment.

"Knock knock." A deep voice whispered, and instantly I knew where I was. Soft footsteps crossed the room, and I heard something being placed on the nightstand. I couldn't face Gage, so I kept the sheets over my head.

"I brought you some aspirin and a glass of water. Take your time getting up. I'm making you hangover food." Gage murmured, then I heard his feet retreating. When the door clicked shut, I exhaled, unaware I'd been holding my breath.

My memories of the prior night were fuzzy. I recalled dancing with Inky and meeting her friends. Oh, and Gage and I kissed—a lot.

"Did we get naked and do something I might regret?" I whispered.

This was worse than the time I got wasted at a frat party in college and woke up naked with a football player. For months I wondered if anything had happened, especially because he was dating a cheerleader who was in one of my classes. Turned out we didn't, but for a long time I was afraid I'd done or said something inappropriate to the guy who'd only felt sorry for me and let me sleep in his bed.

I lowered the sheet and opened my eyes, and then switched on the lamp next to the bed, wincing at the soft light. I lifted the sheet and saw the lacy black panties and bra I'd put on yesterday were still intact. I slid my hand under satin material and gingerly felt around. I didn't feel sore, and if I remembered correctly, there was almost no way Gage could have fucked me and I wouldn't feel it the next day. The last few months of our relationship I'd walked around like I'd just taken up horseback riding, which in a way, I had. Of course, this wasn't proof positive that nothing sexual had happened. Maybe we'd done everything but? It took all of my self-control not to throw myself at Gage every time I saw him, but so far I'd managed it. If I'd been drunk, I was damn sure I'd have found him irresistible.

I drew back the sheet and swung my legs over the side of the bed.

"Jesus, that hurts." I moaned, then examined the floor. No condom wrappers. Then, I remembered the water and pain relievers. He had them on a black, shiny wooden tray. My hands shook as I scooped up the tablets, and moments later I chased them down with the contents of the entire glass, water dribbling down my chin.

"More water, now." I breathed, then looked around the bedroom, praying there was a bathroom adjacent to it, so I didn't have to face the world outside these four walls. There were three doors to choose from, so I tiptoed to the nearest one and opened it to find the biggest closet I'd ever seen in my life. I shut it, crossed the room and tried another one. It opened onto a hallway, and I could smell coffee being brewed. My mouth watered, but I couldn't face Gage hung over wearing only my bra and panties. As I was closing the door I heard footsteps approaching, and Gage whistling softly.

I scrambled to the bed and drew the blankets over me, just as he came into the room.

"Hey, babe, I brought you a big carafe of water, plus coffee and toast." Gage murmured, placing another tray on the nightstand, and grabbing the other one. "You feeling okay?"

"I feel like hell, but I'll survive." Unable to look him in the eye, I reached for the carafe with trembling fingers. Gage placed his hand on mine and I pulled it back.

"I've got this." Gage filled the glass and held it out for me. I drank it down in less than thirty seconds, and I would swear it was the best water I'd had in my life. Gage took the glass from me and refilled it. I downed it faster than the first.

"More?" Gage held up the carafe, and I shook my head, then pointed at the coffee. After a couple of sips, I placed it back on the tray, and finally met Gage's gaze.

"I'm really sorry. Was I a complete mess in front of everyone?" I muttered, praying I had done nothing stupid to embarrass him in front of his guests.

"Nope. All the crazy shit happened after the guests left. Oh, and it wasn't as bad as you think. You want to take a shower while I finish making breakfast? It might make you feel better." Gage's hand lifted, and for a moment I thought he was reaching for me. Instead it fell back to his lap.

"The bathroom is right over there." He said, standing up and pointing to the one door I hadn't tried. "Hope you like pancakes." He grinned, then walked out. When he opened the door, I could smell bacon frying, and my stomach churned. I knew greasy food was good for a hangover, but I was nervous about being able to keep anything down.

When I got out of bed this time, I looked for any evidence that Gage had slept there too, but the sheets, blankets and pillows were all over the place, so I couldn't tell. It mortified me that I'd have to break down and ask him what really happened. With anyone else I would've thrown on my clothes and run out, not worrying about appearances. Not with Gage though, because maybe, just maybe, I wished we'd actually done something, and the naughtier the better.

I was going to put my clothes on from last night, but the food smelled too good, so I threw on Gage's robe which was hanging on the bathroom door. When I walked into the kitchen, Gage began to say something, but then his mouth snapped shut. The coffee he was pouring overflowed the cup.

"Shit!"

I couldn't help but laugh, which hurt like hell, because my head was pounding. A roll of paper towels was on the counter next to me, so I tore off a few sheets and handed them to him. While he mopped up the mess, he glanced my way, biting his lower lip.

"You look so sexy in my robe. Uh, sorry about this." Gage gestured to where he had spilled the coffee, then tossed the towels in the trash can under the sink. "Let me start again." He poured me a cup and handed it to me with a sheepish grin. It was funny to see him blush, something I knew he rarely did.

"Need any help?" I asked. He shook his head and pointed me toward the dining room. Gage followed moments later and set a tray filled with bacon, eggs, pancakes, and syrup on the table. This time my tummy churned with hunger instead of nausea.

"Thanks." I said, and loaded up my plate. Gage was silent. He sipped his orange juice and watched as I made an absolute pig of myself. After last night, I was past the point of embarrassment. When I was done, I piled my dishes on the tray and started for the kitchen.

"You don't have to do that." Gage took the tray out of my hands. When he got to the kitchen he began loading the dishwasher. I picked up a sponge from the sink and was about to start on the counters when he stopped me.

"Please, I've got this. You are my guest."

"I'm surprised you don't have a maid." I teased. I'd had no idea how successful Gage really was, until last night when I discovered he lived in the penthouse. He had never once let on that he was wealthy, his demeanor being so down to earth. His art collection alone must have been worth a healthy chunk of change. Suspicion took hold of my mind; Gage Patterson could have had anyone he wanted, so why the hell did he want me? And why was I resisting?

"I do. Ruthie works Monday through Friday. I can

manage by myself on weekends." Gage replied, a smile starting to spread across his cheeks, but then he looked away.

"Why don't you have a girlfriend?" I blurted, instantly regretting my question. It was none of my business, but it made not a lick of sense. Gage was built like a Greek God, had a swagger that was off the charts hot, and was worth a fortune.

"Because, I've never wanted one before, unless I count what we had ten years ago." He murmured, and I felt something fluttering in my stomach.

"Gage, you don't have to be alone if you don't want to be. I bet you could snap your fingers and get almost anyone you wanted. What's wrong with this picture?"

"Just because I don't have a girlfriend, or have ever contemplated having one, until now, doesn't mean anything is wrong with me. My focus has been on building my business. It doesn't mean I've been a monk, far from it. I've preferred to keep things casual." Gage shut the dishwasher and leaned back against it.

"Lacey, you told me about your botched wedding. You also told me you were never in love with that guy. You could have a second career as a model, and I believe if you snapped your fingers, men would line up around the building to go on a single date with you. What's holding you back?"

I shrugged my shoulders and felt my knees growing weak. Fear held me back, but I wasn't sharing that with him yet. Gage's face grew dark for a moment, then he picked up a rag and started wiping the counter. Moments later, words rushed out of him in a torrent.

"You came on to me last night, Lacey. You're also the one who initiated our first kiss after we had dinner at Beasley's. What that tells me is you're afraid. Of what, I'm not exactly sure." He threw the rag to the side, and faced me. "You still want to have sex? Because if that's all you can handle right now, I'm prepared to keep it light, no strings attached." Gage blushed and put his hands behind his back. I knew what my answer was going to be, but I felt like he had the upper hand, and wasn't sure if I liked that. He'd shared no secrets, yet I'd told him a few.

"I'm sorry about last night, about coming on to you. I shouldn't have drunk so much, but I was nervous about, well, everything." I threw my hands up for a second, then looked away.

"Don't be. I mean, it's not as if I didn't want you to." Gage said, a sly grin spreading across his cheeks. Suddenly, I was incensed. He'd seen me vulnerable, at my very worst. Since we'd reentered each other's lives, I'd told him the gory details of my past. He held the advantage, and my mouth opened before I could think first.

"Do you abuse animals?" I asked. Gage's eyebrows drew together.

"No."

"Do you like to kick people when they're down? Are there any skeletons in your closet I should know about?" I bit off, then his eyes darkened. Gage began to speak, but I attacked even more.

"I've told you my deepest secrets, about Harvard and my fucked-up wedding. It's not fair that I've shared my secrets, but I have none of yours. Have you ever committed a crime? You know, stolen something, or assaulted another person?" I inched closer to him, hoping he'd confess something, anything, so I didn't feel so much like… damaged goods?

"Not that I'm aware of. Why are you asking me these

questions?" Gage crossed his arms over his chest. "I have a feeling your ex ruined your ability to trust men."

I allowed a few seconds to pass, then shrugged my shoulders, and responded, "I don't know why I'm asking them." I sighed. "Maybe to change the subject? I guess I'm a little afraid of you, or more importantly, of us. I don't think I can have a serious relationship with anyone right now. But, I'd be a liar if I said I didn't find you attractive. So, yes, Gage Patterson, I want to have sex with you." I breathed, then closed the distance between us and wrapped my arms around his neck.

His back straightened, and his dark eyes grew wide. For a moment I thought he'd take me there against the kitchen counter. Gage licked his lips and inched forward. I was about to lean in and kiss him, seal the deal so to speak, when he placed his hands on my shoulders and gently pushed. His next words shocked me, but I was also impressed.

"Let's spend the day together first."

Chapter Eleven

GAGE

"I haven't been to the Raleigh Rose Garden since the last time we were here, back in high school." Lacey's head slowly turned, taking in the elegance of the flower beds. It was so quiet, hard to believe the Raleigh Little Theater and the university were only a few yards away. Vibrant pinks, reds, and orange blooms shone under the afternoon sun. "It's even more stunning than I remember."

I didn't speak, wondering if Lacey recalled what we did the last time we'd come here. I'd brought her to the gardens for a reason, hoping to stir up memories of that long-ago day. During spring break, while everyone else in our class vacationed at the beach, we spent the week together exploring the city. This garden was where we'd first exchanged those three magic words. I felt like a teenager again, reliving the same gut-wrenching anxieties I struggled with in my senior year. Summoning the courage to confess how I really felt for the first time wreaked havoc on my emotions. I feared nothing, except rejection. Ten years later, and I still ached to hold her and never let go, yet the same fear persisted. But, if all Lacey wanted was a simple fling, I'd have to honor that.

"Let's sit. I want to enjoy the scenery." Lacey said, then astounded me by reaching for my hand and guiding me to a bench. There was a small pond in front of it, and brightly colored fish swam up to the surface, mouths opening and shutting. It was tough to focus on our surroundings, because a single thought kept dancing through my mind.

Lacey was holding my hand.

"Do you remember what happened here?" Lacey turned in to me and whispered. Was it a trick question? I thought we weren't supposed to be romantic, though holding my hand seemed at odds with her wish to keep things simple. Should I say yes, that I'd never, ever forgotten the first time I'd told her I loved her? Or should I feign ignorance, keeping it light, so it wouldn't seem like I was pressing too hard? I didn't want to freak her out now that her long, delicate fingers were intertwined with mine.

"Of course." I murmured, glancing away. "How could I ever forget?" My eyes couldn't meet hers, because I was afraid she'd see much more than simple lust etched into my features. Lacey's fingers touched my cheek, turning my face until her emerald-green eyes settled on mine

"Gage, I know I've been hard to reach, unable to commit to much. But that doesn't mean I don't remember what we had." Lacey gazed around the pond before her eyes locked with mine once more. "I've never forgotten what took place on this bench all those years ago. No one had ever said they loved me before." Lacey almost looked the same as she did then, except her skin glowed more now, and her face was thinner, more regal, not soft like it once was. There were crinkles at the corners of her eyes, but instead of making Lacey appear older, they added a mature sexiness that made me weak at the knees.

"Wanna do it again? You know, kiss your ex-boyfriend for old times' sake?" Damn it, what the hell had happened to me? If this was anyone else, I would have dragged her back to my apartment for a tumble between the sheets. But with Lacey I had the urge to be something I never was with any other woman—a true gentleman.

"Yes, I'd like nothing more than to kiss you." The way she bit her bottom lip after saying that made my blood heat up. The surrounding gardens disappeared from view when Lacey took my hand in hers and pulled me closer. Then, just like that long-ago afternoon, she shut her eyes. I leaned into her and cupped her face in my palms, letting my lips glance over hers like I did back then. Years ago I had no idea what the hell I was doing. I knew there was more to it than lips touching, but when I was a teenager I worried about fucking it up, so I kept it simple. Drawing back from her, Lacey's eyes opened, wet and glassy. Her lips parted, but instead of kissing her again, I took us back to that far-off day.

"Mom and Dad are going to some fancy shindig at the country club tonight, so we'll have the place to ourselves. Maybe we could play video games and, you know, fool around. Do you think your folks will let you come over?" I whispered. Lacey grabbed my hand and placed it on the curve of her breast.

"There's a payphone in the parking lot. I pissed them off, because I missed curfew last night, and I thought they were going to ground me. I'll butter Mom up, tell her I'll do all the laundry for the next week." Lacey wrapped her arms around my neck and pulled me in tight. Her breath was hot against my skin, and then I felt her tongue playing with my ear, nibbling on the lobe. I shivered, waves of sensation pulsing underneath my cock when she blew in my ear. Placing my hands on her shoulders, I lightly pushed her back.

"Lacey, if I don't get you naked in my bed soon, I will explode in my pants, just like I did that time we made out under the bleachers during that soccer match."

She lifted an eyebrow, got to her feet and reached for my hand.

"Well, we can't have that, can we?"

I didn't want to disappoint Lacey. Halfway home, I wondered if maybe I should have a few minutes of "alone" time in the shower before we advanced any further. My cock was rock hard in my slacks, and when she reached for my hand at a stop light, my foot almost slipped off the brake. There was no way I could satisfy her in this state. It reminded me of the first time we were together, fumbling in the dark of my bedroom. I'd lasted less than a minute. At this point I'd probably shoot my load when I unzipped my pants.

In the elevator I kept my distance, stuffing my hands in my pockets. By the time we arrived on the top floor, Lacey was giving me funny looks.

The keys fell to ground as I attempted to open the door. "Sorry." I mumbled, then Lacey bent down to pick them up. I couldn't keep my eyes off that full round ass I'd been craving since the moment I saw her. With a steadier hand than mine, she fitted the key in the lock.

"After you." Lacey gestured, so I led her inside. When I turned to close the door she was less than a foot away, blocking me.

"Are you still as rough in bed as you used to be?" Lacey said, then pressed herself against me. My mind blanked, then I realized if this was to be a mutually satisfying experience, I had to get myself under control. Hard to do when her hands were in my hair, then on my face, pulling me in for a kiss.

"Lacey, if you don't mind I'm going to grab a quick shower." I kissed her forehead and stepped back.

"Do you want some company?"

Fuck me.

I raked my fingers through my hair. "On the other hand, maybe a mimosa would be good. Yeah, I really want a mimosa."

Lacey's left eyebrow shot up. "Well, I guess a drink would be good. I only want the juice though, no champagne."

Lacey strolled to the balcony windows and stared at the sunset while I raced to the kitchen. I poured her a glass of juice and me a glass of bubbly, skipping the orange juice entirely. When I joined her at the window, I handed Lacey her drink and swallowed half of mine. I tried my best not to look at her, but my pervy mind couldn't keep me from taking half a step back and admiring her from behind.

Why does she have to have the finest ass? It's too perfect. And speaking of perfect, I could see her bra through the thin material of her t-shirt, hiding the most beautiful tits I'd ever seen.

Oh shit, I'm not going to last more than a few seconds.

I raised my glass and finished the other half of my drink. Lacey eyed the empty glass, then looked at her still full one.

"What's wrong?" She murmured, then faced me. The light from the sunset made her pale face glow a luscious golden hue.

"Nothing. I um, you know, everything's good here." I

stammered. She squinted, placing her soft hands on my chest. "It's just, it's been so long since we've been with each other."

"Have you forgotten how to do it?" Lacey asked with a sly smile.

"Of course not, smartass." I bit my lower lip, frustration growing. What the hell was wrong with me? If this was any other woman, I'd have her bent over the railing by now. The way I felt now, if Lacey even rubbed against me I'd lose it.

"It's just like riding a bicycle, except it's much more fun."

I stalked off the balcony to refill my champagne. How the hell would I manage this? When I left the kitchen, Lacey was standing in the living room, pulling her shirt over her head. She obviously worked out, and every lean muscle gleamed in the soft light from the windows. I stopped in my tracks, unable to move or think. Our eyes locked, and she slowly unzipped her jeans, then pulled them off and kicked them across the floor. Her panties and bra were black, lacy, and I wanted nothing more than to rip them off her and smell them, smell her most intimate scent. My mouth watered, then she turned around, lifted her hair, and asked, "Would you unhook my bra?"

Oh my fucking God, she was hot.

I placed my glass on a table and crossed over to her. "Lacey, I don't know if this will be the most satisfying experience. I apologize in advance, because right now I think I'll only last about thirty seconds inside you." Blood rushed to my face, embarrassed at my lack of control.

"I can help you out with that."

Lacey dropped to her knees. Her delicate fingers reached for my zipper, then pulled it down slowly. I laced my fingers through her thick, blonde hair, and pulled her head back so I could gaze into her shimmering green eyes.

"But this is only the beginning, understand?" Lacey murmured, then undid my belt. I grunted, my cock so painfully hard, it throbbed when she pulled it out.

"Jesus, I think you got bigger. Now I'm afraid." She ran her thumb over the crown of my glistening cock, leaking with pre-come. Lacey put her thumb in her mouth, then seconds later I felt her tongue circling the head. I closed my eyes, sparks flying through my brain as her lips closed over it. Lacey folded her hand around the base, and moments later she started an up and down motion with her hand and mouth that immediately had me at the edge.

"Lacey, oh God, I think I'm going to come." I gasped, and tried to pull away.

"Don't stop now. I'll swallow for you." Lacey gave me a wicked grin, then licked the pearl of pre-come that gathered at the tip. My pulse thumped in my ears, then a surge of energy coursed through me. Every ounce of self-control evaporated as the beginning of my orgasm raced up my shaft.

"Take it all baby, I want to feel you take all of me."

My fingers tightened in her hair, and her head bobbed faster while her hand massaged my aching balls. They drew up, and I only had a few seconds before I'd explode. Though she said she would swallow, I had to warn her. Suddenly, her mouth opened wider, and I felt the head of my cock hit the back of her throat.

"Oh God, Lacey, babe, I'm gonna come."

Her head nodded, never missing a beat as her throat pulled the come out of my shaft. My mind filled with images of us fucking, of me taking her on her knees, on top of me, below me, in every fucking position.

"Here it comes."

Lacey grabbed my ass as come fired out of my cock. I

bent over her, unable to breathe, while her hand and mouth massaged every drop out of me. Then her hand slid back to my balls and gave a little squeeze, and seconds later her mouth left my cock. I fell to my knees. Shit, that had to be the best orgasm of my fucking life. She'd gained some skills over the years, and my dick was very happy about it.

Gathering me in her arms, Lacey held me while I regained my strength. Her hands feathered through my hair, then she pulled me back for a kiss. The taste of her lips drove me insane, and despite the intensity of my orgasm, I felt my cock stirring.

"Lacey, that was crazy what you did to me. That was—"

"Only the start." She interrupted. "There's more to come, trust me."

Chapter Twelve

LACEY

"Let me take them off." Gage's eyes were like saucers as he fell to his knees in front of me. "I've wanted to taste you since you walked back into my life."

Moments later, my panties were around my ankles.

Gage kissed the inside of my thigh. "One foot at a time, step out of them."

I did as he said, then he commanded, "Sit down, and spread your legs as wide as you can."

I sat on the edge of the bed, but when I went to spread my legs open for him, I suddenly felt shy, too exposed.

"Open those legs wide for me, Lacey." He murmured. My heart raced, and my first instinct was to do the opposite, but I swallowed my insecurities and did as he asked.

A cocky grin spread across Gage's face, then he licked his lips and buried his face against me, and I gasped.

"Gage," I hissed, and his tongue slid from one end of me to the other, then he flicked it across my swollen clit. Any hesitation I'd had earlier flew out the window as he sucked my clit. I dug my fingers into his hair, moaning his name while my hips began to writhe.

"Oh, God, Gage." I moaned, and felt a tear sliding down my cheek. It felt so amazing, then I jerked when he thrust his tongue inside me.

"I want to taste everything you have to give, make you come for me, Lacey." Gage said, his voice vibrating the tender flesh as he spoke. My entire body trembled, then Gage worked his tongue back to my engorged clit. Two of his fingers slid inside of me, and I felt overwhelmed by all the sensations he was creating, then I heard Gage groan.

"Come on my tongue babe." He said, the vibrations of his words directly against my clit. My fingers dug into his hair, and I felt Gage's fingers lifting my ass, then holding me in place while his tongue worked its magic. His fingers curled up inside of me and he increased the suction.

"Jesus, Gage, you're going to make me come." My voice was so high, it almost sounded like a screech, and then an orgasm tore through me, so hard it bordered on violence. My body shook as Gage massaged the sensitive spot inside of me, and he didn't stop until I practically collapsed against the bed. I panted, unable to form words and my eyes snapped shut. My body felt weightless, and stars danced beneath my closed eyelids.

I heard Gage stand up, then he was next to me on the bed, scooping me into his arms as I came down from the electric high he'd created. His body slid behind mine and I could feel his length hard against my ass.

"I want to make love to you, Lacey, but I also want to do vile, filthy things too. I want you on all fours, and to take you from behind, one hand on your beautiful tits as I slide my cock deep inside you." His voice sounded like gravel, deep and rough, and I wondered if I could come again just by hearing him talk dirty to me. Gage's erection pressed hard into my skin, and I knew I had to have him as deep inside me as our bodies would allow.

My body began to vibrate, knowing that the orgasm I'd had earlier was only a prelude to what was yet to come. My former fiancé had never made me come like this. In fact, no one had, except for Gage. I turned over and faced him, wanting to see his dark, sultry eyes. I glanced down and saw his cock straining between us. He had every reason to be cocky about his skills in bed, and I reached down and squeezed his girth.

Without warning, he hoisted me up the bed until my head was on the pillows, and he lay on top of me. Gage brushed my hair off my forehead and kissed it.

"Feeling good?" He smirked, provoking a cascade of giggles from me. "Because, we can stop now, or we can do what I want, which is bury myself in you."

Unable to form a complete sentence, I bit my lower lips and nodded. A huge grin slowly split his face, then he reached over and opened the drawer of his nightstand, and pulled out a box of condoms. After snatching one out he tossed the box to the floor and ripped open the package with his teeth. After sliding it on he locked his gaze with mine and smiled.

"This is a dream come true." He murmured, and I felt my own smile spreading across my face. Our smiles triggered a change in the atmosphere, and I felt the connection between us growing more intense. Then, Gage gently worked his length inside me, slow measured thrusts as he eased in and out. He was large, and once my body accepted his size, he pushed inside a little deeper, and harder, and once he had filled me completely, a high-pitched moan escaped my throat.

My hips met each of his thrusts until a rhythm developed, and the sounds and smells of sex filled the air. A sheen of sweat covered Gage's face, then he shifted his body and lifted my leg, ever so slightly changing the angle of his thrusts, until he found my tender spot inside.

"Oh, Gage…"

His stubbled jaw flexed, almost as if he were angry, and I realized it was because he was holding back, wanting me to climax before he finished himself. Something about his caring about my needs triggered my body, and I felt an orgasm building deep inside, and my eyes fluttered shut.

"Open them, babe, I want to see your eyes when you come all over my cock." Gage sped up the tempo of his thrusts, and my eyes snapped open and locked with his gaze. My entire frame shook as I clenched down on his length. The intensity of his gaze was nearly overwhelming, but the hard glint of his dark eyes held me in thrall as my climax rocketed through my body.

Gage smiled down at me as my orgasm ebbed, then his arm and chest muscles tightened, and he began to fuck me, hard. The headboard smacked the wall repeatedly, until his body went completely still, and a roar ripped out of his throat.

His arms shook, and he collapsed on top of me, kissing my cheeks, then my hair as he continued to gently glide his length in and out. I didn't want the moment to end, loving the connection we'd created between us, but then he had to deal with the condom, so he eased out of me and got off the bed.

Gage padded into the bathroom, and as he did the air

conditioning kicked on, and the jolt of cold air blowing against my sweat-soaked skin created a chill, and my brain suddenly reeled at the thought of what had just happened.

No one had ever fucked me like that before, not even Gage when we were teenagers. And I feared that if this connection between us deepened any further, I was going to be fucked in an emotional way that could possibly tear me apart.

Chapter Thirteen

GAGE

Hours passed and Lacey's head remained on my chest, her arm flung over my stomach. I shifted slightly so I wouldn't wake her, one of my legs tingling from being in the same place for too long. Contentment washed through me as I listened to the gentle sound of her breathing. Lacey's eyes danced under her lids, and I wondered what she was dreaming about, if perhaps she ever dreamed about me?

Fuck.

How could I keep things light now that she'd walked back into my life? For years I'd never been interested in anything more than casual sex, but with Lacey I was unsure I could keep things strings-free. My eyes fluttered shut, and I recalled the vow, that idealistic promise we'd made to each other that long-ago night when we went our separate ways.

"In ten years' time, if we both are still single, let's meet at our high school reunion, and maybe we can…"

"I promise you, Gage, in ten years we will be together, though I don't know how I'm going to wait so long."

Was it possible I was still in love with her?

When you were a kid, ten years seemed like a lifetime, but now that all those years had passed, it felt like only yesterday that my heart was torn into a million tiny pieces. A tear coursed down my cheek, and I swiped at it with the back of my hand. Fuck me, this was the second time she'd made me cry since she'd returned. I hadn't shed any tears since that night ten years ago, and here I was becoming a crybaby whenever she was around. Since the moment I'd seen Lacey at the hospital when Dad was sick, I'd been wrecked, to the point I barely recognized myself any longer.

If this had been one of my usual casual fucks, I would have offered them a warm towel and shown them the door by now, but this wasn't just anybody. Lacey had the power to either complete me, or utterly demolish the life I'd created for myself. But, if all she wanted was a sexual thing, friends with benefits, or whatever they called it nowadays, I was game. However, I couldn't stop hoping that she felt the same way for me that I felt for her.

My eyelids grew heavy. I hated to do it, but now my other leg was cramping, so I carefully turned over, praying I wouldn't wake Lacey.

"I'm not asleep, Gage. You okay?" She yawned, then wrapped her arm around me and kissed my back.

I debated whether I should tell her the truth. Would Lacey freak out if she knew how I actually felt? No, I couldn't risk it.

"I'm okay, just reminiscing. Thinking about our school

days, that's all." I squeezed her hand and held it against my chest. My heart thumped underneath, and I hoped she didn't notice it ramping up.

"Oh, I hated high school. When I transferred there for junior year, I thought it would be miserable, filled with the usual high-school cliques. Then, I met you, and everything changed." Lacey murmured, her breath tickling the hairs on the back of my head.

"Did I ever tell you about flunking that Latin test on purpose?" I snickered.

"What are you talking about?"

"You were the new kid, acing all of your papers. I knew Mr. Creighton would get you to tutor me, you know, to help you make friends. I'd tutored a classmate the year before, so I figured he'd do the same thing. Plus, I was a straight-A student, so it freaked him out that I'd flunked a test... oh, and I skipped out on some homework too. That's how I got us quality time alone in the school library." I laughed. Damn, I was a determined kid. Lacey laughed too, thank God. For a moment I worried she'd think I'd been a stalker since day one.

"Whatever Gage wants, he gets, right?" Lacey tightened her grip on me, and I felt soft kisses on my back. Fuck it, maybe I could take this further than I thought.

"You know what else I remember? That promise we made to each other, while strolling around Lake Johnson." I murmured, and waited for a response. When I got none, I continued, "If ten or so years passed and we were both still single, we'd find each other. I promised you I'd wait forever." I whispered the last sentence, and when she didn't respond, my gut twisted into a knot.

Shit. My fucking big mouth was getting me in trouble again, scaring her off.

I waited for Lacey to speak, and every second stretched into an eternity. I fully expected her to leap out of the bed and race for the door.

Instead, the sound of her soft snores put my nerves at rest. Thank God she hadn't heard me. I settled back on the pillow and closed my eyes, our first kiss playing over and over in my mind.

The sunrise woke me from a dead sleep, so I leapt out of bed to shut the drapes, hoping she wasn't awakened by the light. When I turned around, I realized I shouldn't have bothered.

Lacey was gone.

Chapter Fourteen

LACEY

"If ten or so years passed, and we were both still single, we'd find each other. I promised you I'd wait forever." Gage whispered, and I froze.

The night was perfect. Romantic and sexy fun, just what the doctor ordered, but then Gage had to bring up The Promise. Oh my God, I hadn't thought of that in years, though of course I'd never forgotten it.

When I was kicked out of Harvard Medical School, that promise kept me going as I struggled to move forward with my life. If all else failed, maybe Gage would be the pot of gold at the end of the rainbow. I grappled with the decision to move home with my tail between my legs, but decided against it. How could I face the humiliation of being booted out of one of the finest universities in the world? What would my friends and family say? Would Gage be ashamed of me, shun me for being a loser? Or even worse, had he moved on with another woman?

But, life carried on, and eventually I found a way through the pain. I dated other men, had crushes, almost married a rich doctor for all the wrong reasons. The promise was real. It represented the love we had, and that we would always have for each other, even if it was in the distant future. Now that future was here, and it scared the hell out of me.

Gage shifted, and I thought he might be waiting for my response. God help me, I faked snoring, hoping he'd stop bringing up the past, which was rapidly becoming the present. I knew he wasn't proposing marriage, but it sounded like he wanted to take our friends-with-benefits situation and elevate it to a higher level, and I wasn't prepared for that. Once I was sure he was asleep, I'd escape. As amazing as it was to feel his arms around me, to feel him inside me again after all these years, I couldn't handle anything serious with him, or anyone else.

"Somebody looks like they stayed up all night. Hope it was fun." Powell elbowed me in the side and smirked. I could feel blood rushing to my face, and Powell bit his lip to keep from laughing.

"It was… fun." Hell, there was no way I could forget it. I was sore from the serious fucking I had received last night. It was a good kind of sore that made me smile instead of wince. That was tempered by the text message I received from Gage this morning. He said he was sorry if he made me uncomfortable, that he wanted to make it up to me.

That made me wince.

I hadn't replied, not knowing what to say. Despite my reservations, I didn't want to hurt him. He was my first love, and even if he made me want to bang my head against the wall with his headstrong ways, causing him pain was not on my agenda.

"You're a fast worker. Was it that stud who came to see you last week?"

"Jesus, Powell. What's up with all the questions? Yes, I was with him."

"Sorry. Jeez, you're touchy today. Just moved back to Raleigh and you've already got yourself a boyfriend. Wish I could be so lucky." Powell muttered. I faked a laugh, then we were confronted by the arrival of a young mother with her son.

"Please, you gotta help my baby. A bunch of thugs beat him up. I think his arm is broken." Tears coursed down her cheeks, though I could tell she was trying to keep it together for her child's sake. He couldn't have been more than twelve years old, his somber face hiding his pain. Both were trying to be strong for the other, and it wasn't working.

"I'll take him to the examination room. Powell, would you mind getting her information?" I asked, then crouched in front of the youngster.

"It's going to be alright. What's your name?"

"Tommy. Tommy Jenkins." He tilted his chin up defiantly, but I noticed his eyes were red and glassy, one almost swollen shut. Not only was his arm possibly broken, but he had a black eye, and a bloody crust was forming around his nostrils.

"We're going to get you cleaned up, and I'll get the doctor to see you as soon as possible. I want you to follow me now, Tommy, okay?"

"You're a lucky young man." Doctor Nash said. "One of your bones, the ulna, had a clean break. Most likely it won't require resetting, but you will be wearing that sling for a few weeks. Ms. Barnes here will send you home with instructions on home care."

"Thank you, sir." Tommy replied, and the doctor left. His mother burst into tears again, reached out to hug him, then stopped, afraid of hurting him.

"Oh, baby, don't ever get in the way of a bunch of bullies like that again. Run, crawl, do whatever it takes to get away." The mother, Latrice Jenkins, was distraught over much more than her son's arm though. Before I brought her back to the examination room, she asked me about the bill, and from the look in her eye I knew it was going to be an issue.

"I'm going to see to your paperwork and will be back in a flash. You two stay here while I get things taken care of." Mrs. Jenkins gingerly wrapped her arms around Tommy as I left the room. I needed to get their forms ready, but I also needed Powell's help. I was still new, and unfamiliar with any programs the hospital had for patients who struggled financially. It was obvious the woman would do anything for her son, and it tore me up inside to think money stood in the way of Tommy getting the best care possible.

"Powell, are you with someone right now?" He shook his head no.

"I need your help with that mother and son who came in with the broken arm. From what Mrs. Jenkins said, they are struggling financially and I don't know enough about hospital policy to..."

"I've got it. Get their paperwork together, oh, and you're going to need this too." He reached under the counter, then placed a form on the stack I already had. "Come with me, so you can learn what to say the next time this happens." Powell walked briskly to the exam room with me hurrying to keep up.

"Mrs. Jenkins?" Powell said, when he opened the blue curtain.

"Yes, but you can call me Latrice." She held out her hand which Powell shook.

"Tommy, I'm going to borrow your mother for a few minutes. Will you be okay on your own?" He asked. The boy nodded, and we left. Powell led us to the empty gray office at the end of the corridor.

"Normally someone from finance would go over this with you, but seeing that you've been through so much already I'm not going to make you wait. Lacey told me you had concerns about the bill." He said once the three of us were seated. She nodded, then brushed a tear away. Poor woman's eyes were so swollen it had to be painful.

"We have several options to help you. UNC Rex Hospital takes pride in treating everyone regardless of their ability to pay. What I'm going to do is set you up with an appointment to speak with a social worker who will help you with financial arrangements. Is it okay for me to do that?"

She nodded, her back straightening. I sensed she was uncomfortable talking about her finances.

"Tommy is enrolled in Medicaid, and I get him regular checkups through the city health department. I do my best to keep my boy healthy. What on earth was he thinking getting in the middle of that mess?" She shook her head and put her face in her hands for a moment, taking a couple of deep breaths.

"Is this the best number where we can reach you?" Powell

asked, a note of concern in his voice. Latrice nodded, and her left leg bounced up and down from nerves.

"I will take care of it on my end. You will be contacted in one to three days to inform you about the appointment I'm setting up with the social worker. Now if you could sign these forms…" Powell spoke in a steady, calm voice as he explained all she needed to do to keep Tommy's arm comfortable at home, and about the financial aid programs. Powell impressed me with his caring professionalism. By the time he was through she managed a small smile, then asked where the nearest bus stop was.

I was nearing the end of my shift, and something about Latrice and Tommy touched me. This woman was trying so damn hard to be the best Mom she could be, and it must seem like the world was throwing every obstacle it could in her path.

"I'm about to leave myself. Would you like a ride?" I blurted out. Powell raised an eyebrow, but Latrice turned to me with the first real smile I'd seen from her since she arrived.

"Oh, if it's no trouble, that would be wonderful."

"Give me twenty minutes and I'll get you both home." I glanced at her address on the form. It was only ten minutes from my place downtown. "You're practically right down the street from me. It's no trouble at all."

Latrice and Tommy lived off Capital Boulevard in a rundown apartment complex called the Millbrook Arms. When they got out of the car, the door to the rental office flew open and a tall man with shoulder-length gray hair ran over.

"There you are. I've been worried sick about you." The man cried. Latrice flew into his arms while Tommy stood back respectfully.

"Mr. Parker, you have no idea what we've…"

"I know exactly what you've been through. Those men who've been sabotaging the building beat the crap out of Tommy." The man crouched down in front of the boy and examined his broken arm.

"You were very brave confronting those men. But don't you dare do that again. Mrs. Hernandez in 2C called me right after it happened. She saw the whole thing, told me you saw them sneaking around the back to the basement. Said they had a big saw with them. They were bad men, but it's not your responsibility to fight them. Next time, you run away and then call the police." He stood up and sighed. Then he noticed me leaning against my car.

"You're wearing scrubs. Did you help this young man today?"

"Yes, I gave them a ride home from the hospital. Sounds like Tommy here is a brave guy, but I'm with you. He should never, ever fight with a bunch of grown men. What's going on? Were they burglars?" I replied, curious as to why grown men would beat on a kid.

"A few months ago, a real estate developer made me an offer to buy this place. I refused. This place is home for so many people I'm proud to call my friends. Since then I've had my basement flooded, the furnace broke down, though it was only two years old, and the electrical boxes were overloaded. They've made four offers, each better than the last, but I've turned them all down. Every time I say no, another so-called accident happens. A man with the real-estate agency was here last week, and of course the thugs came back. These shady developers are trying to run us out of the neighborhood to build more of their overpriced lofts and fancy nightclubs. I'm not selling, no matter what they do." He turned and addressed Tommy again. "I'm telling you once more. If you see some shady characters around here, hide. They know who you are now, kid." Tommy shrugged his shoulders and turned to his mom.

"Can we have Chinese takeout for dinner? I'm starving."

Latrice's face collapsed for a brief second, then she mustered a smile. After her talk with Powell earlier about finances, I had a feeling she would have to tell him no. After the day he'd had, I thought he deserved a treat.

"Actually, I'm hungry too. Point me to the nearest takeout and I'll get you whatever you want."

"No, you don't have to do that!" Latrice exclaimed, and I saw her eyes fill up with tears again. The woman had been through it today, and I felt my eyes getting wet too.

"I insist. Tommy deserves it, and so do you. So, what can I get for you both?"

"Aunt Millie. What are you doing here?" My aunt surprised me by pulling into the parking lot as I was getting out of my car.

"Happy Family has the best WonTon soup in Raleigh. I'm hungry, what else would I be doing here?" She hugged me. "This is a little out of your way. How'd you find out about it?"

I explained to her about what happened with the Jenkins

family. She'd worked as a community activist for years, and her eyes dimmed as she heard about what Tommy had gone through.

"Those assholes." She said, taking me by surprise. I'd never heard her curse before. "The same thing happens all over town, whenever those rich sons of bitches drive poorer families out of their homes. Gentrification is a fancy name for kicking out the 'undesirables.' Then they have the nerve to complain about the homeless. How the hell do they think some of the homeless became that way in the first place?" She grabbed me by the arm and dragged me into the restaurant. "I'm taking care of this. What are they eating?"

Half an hour later the two of us delivered their dinners. We found the Jenkins family and Mr. Parker on a playground behind the building. They were waiting for us at an old picnic table, its green paint peeling off. Latrice greeted us shyly as we approached.

"My son and I appreciate all you've done for us today." She took a bag from my hand and set it down. "People like you give us hope. That's hard to come by nowadays. Tommy, run inside and wash up before you eat. Oh, and be careful with…" By the time she got to the end of her sentence he was inside the building. Latrice laughed and shook her head. "He's a handful, but he's my everything."

Aunt Millie and I placed the other bags on the table, and Mr. Parker helped.

"My name is Millie. I ran into my niece at Happy Family, the Chinese place." She introduced herself to Mr. Parker, who shook her hand for a second longer than usual. "Bruce Parker. I own the place. I assume your niece told you about what's been going on here. Tommy was a brave fool today, but I have to admit if more people would stick up for what's right, this world would be a better place." Aunt Millie beamed, and if my eyes weren't deceiving me, she was blushing.

I took a closer look at Bruce, then at her, wondering if a love connection was happening in front of my eyes. Once they filled their plates they sat next to each other, neither saying much, but that didn't last for long. Minutes later their food remained untouched as they talked passionately about corruption at City Hall.

"Latrice," I said, after finishing my meal. "This is my phone number. If you need anything at all please call me." I scribbled my number on an old business card I found in my wallet. "And, I'm not just saying that. If Tommy needs a ride to a doctor's appointment, or you just need to talk, let me know." It had been a long day, and I was ready to be in my own bed. "Aunt Millie, I'm leaving now. Are you going to be okay?"

"Thank you, hon, but Bruce is going to show me some of his artwork. I can see myself home." Her hand rested on his forearm. I kissed her cheek and shook Bruce's hand, who barely glanced at me, since he couldn't take his eyes off of her.

As I walked to my car I thought about the text message Gage had sent earlier this morning. Before I started the car I glanced at my phone, debating whether I should send him a message back. I thought about the instant attraction my aunt and Bruce seemed to share, and wondered what was stopping me from giving in to my own desires.

It would be a lie to say I didn't feel those old feelings for Gage stirring inside. He was everything I ever wanted in a man, but damn it, the thought of being hurt again scared the hell out of me. Aunt Millie's husband had died years ago, and apparently she was ready for romance. My disastrous relationship with Ted only ended a few months ago, and I was unsure about, well, anything related to love.

I backed the car out of the parking lot and had the sudden urge to keep driving, to flee up the interstate until I ran out of gas. When I looked at my hands on the steering wheel my knuckles were white from gripping it so hard. Damn it, it wasn't that I didn't love Gage, it was just… oh my God.

Did I just admit that I loved him?

By the time I walked into my apartment building, I'd decided not to text Gage. I wouldn't leave him hanging for long, but I needed a little more space to figure out what I wanted. Plus, a long hot bath and a glass of Merlot was sounding like the perfect antidote to this very long day.

When the elevator doors opened I detected a sweet and spicy aroma, and when I turned the corner I knew why; a huge bouquet of red and white roses was in front of my door. It was in an elaborate jade vase I immediately recognized from his living room.

"You are killing me, Gage." I murmured as I entered the apartment. When I set the flowers on the coffee table, I noticed a tiny white card attached. Dread filled me. Today had been sooo long, and the thought of dealing with anything serious made my stomach churn. My fingers trembled as I opened the little envelope, but after I read it, all I could do was fall back on the couch and laugh.

Roses are red
I'm feeling blue

Let's keep it simple

Please let me fuck you

I was still sore from our romp last night, but the thought of him doing what he'd done to me all over again made me instantly wet. I raced to the bedroom and opened the closet to find something else to wear. Then it struck me; why was I bothering? He was only a short elevator ride away. I yanked off my scrubs and grabbed my robe off the hook in the bathroom. I was going there for one reason only; a good fucking. Before we did it though, I'd set the ground rules; no love, just sex.

When I passed the roses on my way to leave, I stopped in my tracks. What the hell was I thinking? Remember what he said last night? The promise? I snatched the card off the table and read it through twice.

"Fuck it." I muttered, then I tossed the card in the air and raced for the door.

With an invitation like that, how could I refuse?

Chapter Fifteen

GAGE

I paced the living room in my bare feet, and a glass of wine I'd poured an hour earlier remained untouched. Lacey had to be home by now, and must have discovered the roses and the card. I'd sat at my desk all day working on that silly poem. Whenever Dad came into the office to yell at me, I'd hide it under my paperwork, barely able to focus on anything he said.

Countless sappy love poems were balled up in the trash can under the desk, and it wasn't until the day was almost over that I realized a heartfelt declaration of love was the last thing Lacey would want. I'd already ordered the roses and would not let them go to waste, but instead of romantic words, I scribbled out that silly poem on the tiny white card, hoping to make her laugh. She hadn't knocked on my door, so I had a suspicion it didn't work.

Fuck my stupid heart. Maybe I had to accept the fact that it was over between us. My stupid fantasy of picking up where we left off was just that, stupid. Lacey was a different woman than she was back then. Hell, we were kids ten years ago. Neither of us had a clue about the real world, and I needed to admit to myself that she didn't want me for anything else but a tumble between the sheets now and then.

I snatched up my glass of wine and downed its contents. Instead of refilling it, I put the empty glass in the sink and snatched a tumbler from the cabinet. Scotch was what this situation called for.

"I can't do this." I said out loud, then gulped my drink, relishing the burn as the amber liquid filled my throat. "Friends with benefits? It can't happen. There's no way I can sleep with her and keep things casual."

I was about to refill the tumbler when there was a knock at the door.

"Well, holy shit, she's either here to fuck, or to tell me to fuck off." I whispered, not knowing if I could honestly handle either of those scenarios. Paralyzed by dread, I couldn't move my feet. Another soft knock on the door, and I was frozen in place.

"Stop being such a wuss, Gage Patterson." I muttered, then slapped my cheek.

My feet finally moved. When I opened the door no one was there. I stepped out of the doorway and looked down the hall. Lacey was standing in her bathrobe by the elevator.

"Hey, you." I called out, and I was hit with a jolt of dizziness. Her face lit up, and I felt the vertigo slip away.

"I thought no one was home." She replied. A second later, she was draping her hands around my neck.

"The roses were beautiful, and the card…" Lacey laughed, "...it was perfect. I had a long-ass day, and I needed the laugh." She pecked me on the lips.

"Glad I could make you smile, Lacey. I live for…"

"Before you go any further, I need to make something perfectly clear."

"What's that?"

"Let's be friends. I can't handle anything serious right now. If you can agree to that, I'll come inside. Otherwise, I need to head back downstairs. Are you able to keep things light and simple? Because your invitation was pretty clear about wanting to sleep with me, and I'd love nothing more than to let you." Lacey leaned in and kissed the side of my neck. My thoughts raced, unable to formulate an answer, one of the few times in my life I'd struggled to find the correct words. Could I really keep things simple? My heart pounded against my ribcage, and I realized if all I could have was this, her body warm against mine on occasion, I'd have to accept it or have no part of Lacey at all.

I stepped to the side and my voice cracked.

"Come inside, Lacey."

"You have nothing on under that robe, I bet." I whispered. I stood at the bedroom door, paralyzed with fear. Lacey had been walking toward the bed, but stopped in her tracks. She spun around slowly, a cautious smile spreading across her face.

"Come here and let me show you."

The muscles in my legs tightened, and I felt beads of sweat rolling down my side. My feet wouldn't budge. I was so afraid of saying or doing the wrong thing. I wanted nothing more than to make love to Lacey, but I wasn't sure if 'making love' was what she wanted. I'd give anything to make Lacey want me the way I wanted her, but at the very least I could pretend that her heart was open to mine.

Lacey's hands moved to her waist, and moments later the cool blue fabric of her robe fell to the floor.

"Jesus." I murmured, and I felt my hands grow clammy. She stood there, head down, then raised it and our eyes locked. Lacey blushed, and I felt my heart lurch. Lacey closed the distance between us until she stood inches away, her nose practically brushing mine. All I could think was how madly, truly, deeply I felt love for this woman. How could I keep my feelings out of it?

"You are so handsome, Gage Patterson. But you'd look even hotter with your clothes off." Lacey whispered, and started unbuttoning my shirt. I said nothing, unable to take my eyes off her long, nimble fingers as they undressed me. Once she was done Lacey laid her warm palms on my chest, leaned in and placed her lips on mine. My mouth opened, and my body finally acted like the only woman I'd ever wanted was touching me, wanting me. Her lips tasted sweet, and her tongue swirling around mine made my wildly beating heart speed up even more.

"Off with those pants." Lacey breathed, breaking the kiss and stepping back. I kicked off my loafers and with fumbling fingers, I managed to unbutton my slacks. Lacey dropped to her knees and pulled my underwear and pants to my ankles. She rubbed her forehead against my cock, then licked the underside of my balls. Electricity raced through my limbs, and when she finally took my cock in her mouth, my knees quaked.

"Oh yes, God, Lacey, this is…" I moaned, then words failed me. My eyes snapped shut and I weaved my fingers through her thick blonde hair. Lacey's hand worked the base of my shaft while her tongue swirled around the crown. My legs shook, and for a moment I wondered if I would fall to the floor. Abruptly, Lacey stopped and got to her feet.

"Bed." She murmured, then took me by the hand. "Lie down, Gage."

I obeyed. Lacey walked to my closet door and entered it. I was about to ask why, when she walked out with a plain black tie in her hand.

"What are you doing?"

"It's your turn to be vulnerable." Lacey straddled my chest and placed the fabric over my eyes. "Lift up for a sec." She tied it around my head, and the world went black. Shit, if she only knew just how fucking vulnerable I already was.

I felt Lacey's knees shift and soon the spicy scent of her pussy filled my nostrils.

"Oh God, Lacey." I murmured, then my tongue snaked out for a taste, and Lacey gasped. Her body quaked, and moments later my lips found her clit and began sucking and licking.

"Yes, Gage." Lacey groaned. I felt her hips shaking as my tongue tasted her essence, and though I wanted to feel her coming on my lips, I also wanted to be inside of her, deep inside her.

"Wait, oh God." Lacey pulled her pussy away from my mouth, and I was unable to tell what she wanted, thanks to the blindfold. I felt her lean to the side and heard the drawer to the nightstand slide open. Seconds later she scooted down the bed and parted my legs. She placed a slicked up hand on my shaft, lubing it up, then I felt a condom rolling down my length. Lacey climbed on top and her hands positioned my dick against her entrance.

"You know what to say now, don't you?" She asked, her

voice thick like syrup. I wracked my brain, trying to figure out what she wanted me to say, then my mouth opened and I spat out the word.

"Please."

Lacey pushed down and I felt the first couple of inches slide in before she grew still, her breathing labored. My hands gripped her waist, wanting to push her all the way down, but I resisted the urge. She wanted to be in control. It struck me while I lay beneath her unable to see her face, that this was what the blindfold was really about, whether she knew it consciously or not.

Lacey needed to be in control, because she was afraid—of what I didn't know.

I felt her fingers on my nipples, her breathing ragged while she became used to my size, then she went all the way down on my cock. Sheer energy raced through me, and the desire to flip her over and take her the way I liked it, the way I knew she loved it, overwhelmed me.

"Lacey, I don't think I can..." I started to say, then her lips crushed against mine and I gasped in shock.

"Lie back, enjoy the ride, Gage." Lacey murmured as she pulled away.

Lacey leaned back and then her pace quickened, her tight wet pussy working my cock furiously. I'd never been blindfolded during sex before, and not being able to see her face while she rode my cock frustrated me, but I knew she needed to feel in control.

Every time she sank all the way down my shaft a hit of euphoria flashed through my body. Lacey's pussy was so tight, and the way it gripped my cock was sending me closer to the point of no return.

"Oh God, Gage, I'm really close. I'm…" Lacey began, then I lost control.

"Lacey, I have to… fuck." I said through gritted teeth, then I reached up and ripped the tie from my eyes. Lacey's eyes were shut as she rode my cock, unaware that I'd torn the blindfold off. I gripped her sides and lifted her off, then flipped Lacey onto her back.

"Gage, what are you doing?" Lacey's eyes widened.

"I gotta take you darling, the way you and I love it best. Rough and hard babe, rough and hard." I slammed my cock in to the hilt.

"Yes, oh God, Gage." Lacey moaned, her eyes rolling back. Over and over I impaled her, her hips bucking to meet my cock as I pulled it almost all of the way out then rammed it back in. Moments later Lacey's eyes snapped shut and her pussy tightened its grip on my cock.

"Gage, oh Gage." She moaned, and she went perfectly still as her orgasm rolled through her body.

"That's it, babe, tighter. You're squeezing the come out of my cock with your beautiful pussy." I muttered, then moaned her name as my orgasm throbbed through my groin. My knees shook, throwing me off balance. Unable to hold myself up I fell against her, my face landing on her shoulder with a soft smack.

"Where did you learn to…?" Lacey's voice trailed off as we both gasped for air. We lay like that for more than a minute, and then I lifted my face and licked her neck, then brushed my lips over hers. Lacey opened her eyes and giggled.

"What's so funny?"

"Nothing. Everything. Gage, that was incredible." Her green eyes locked with mine, then another giggle escaped her lips. Moments later I felt laughter bubbling up my throat, and then I rolled over, lay on my back, and we both laughed for a good minute or two. Finally we both grew quiet and she laid her head on my chest.

"Thank you, Gage." She whispered, and then we curled into each other and fell asleep, limbs tangled, and my inner thoughts of love were silenced, if only for a while.

Lacey shifted in my arms, and I opened my eyes from a dreamless slumber. I pulled her tighter into my chest, wanting her soft skin warm against mine. Then I kissed her hair and inhaled her seductive scent. A strange sensation of peace filled me, almost like my heart would explode in my chest. Having Lacey in my arms again was such a fucking miracle, something I never expected to happen after all our time apart. Then, the opposite of peace hit, anxiety taking its place. Despite my iron grip on Lacey, I was terrified of her slipping away.

"I love you." I mouthed into Lacey's back, not making a sound. She might not want to hear it, but my mouth needed to form the words.

Chapter Sixteen

LACEY

Gage's lips were parted, and his eyes were shut. The look on his face pulled me back in time to when we were teenagers. The years had been kind to Gage, but the peacefulness of sleep stripped the age from his face, rendering him a horny seventeen-year-old again. Damn, even asleep he looked like a cocky devil.

I turned over on my stomach, and propped my chin up on my hands, noticing that the skin around my mouth felt scratchy and rough. Gage's dark scruff was the culprit, and a smile spread across my face. I wanted his mouth on mine again, and felt myself getting wet.

Was I falling in love with him again?

Gage shifted in his sleep, then turned on his side, where I couldn't see his face. His back was as chiseled as his front, and without thinking it through, I scooted into his side, and threw my arm around his waist, hugging him tight.

"Somebody's happy to see me this morning." Gage drawled, then he turned over and the look in his eyes nearly took my breath away. It wasn't his usual lusty stare, but instead it was a serene gaze, filled with contentment. His hand wrapped around the back of my neck and pulled me to his lips. The burn of his scruff on my raw skin made me forget about morning breath, or the need to brush my teeth first. Every self-conscious protest I'd normally make, had faded from my mind with that one, simple kiss. When he pulled away, his fingers feathered over my neck, then inched into my hair sending shivers up and down my spine.

"Lacey, your face haunts my thoughts, and your eyes make me want to tie you to this bed right now, so you can never…" Gage's lips snapped shut and he withdrew his fingers from the back of my head. Sitting up against the pillows, he stretched and yawned. His words made me smile, but only on the inside. Damn it, Gage, I needed this to be simple, but I knew deep down it was going to be impossible with him.

"Gage..." I whispered, "...if I didn't have to be at work in an hour, I'd handcuff myself to the bed. Oh, and I think maybe you've been in a few of my dreams too." I murmured, then reached under the blanket and grasped his dick in my hand, giving it a gentle tug. "Want to tie me up tonight?" I asked, then stuck my head under the blanket and licked the head of his cock.

"Shit, Lacey, if you keep doing that, neither of us will make it out of this bed today. Yes, of course, tonight. You don't have to ask twice." Gage threw the blankets off. I got on my knees and kissed the tip of his nose.

"It's a date."

Despite the threat of tying me up that morning, no restraints were necessary that evening. Gage met me at the door buck naked, and in less than a minute so was I. Now that we'd satisfied our carnal hunger, both of us were starving. A pizza was ordered, and we opened a bottle of Merlot to drink with it, while we devoured the pie on the balcony. Sex must have burned a lot of calories, because we ate like it was the first meal we'd had in days. Gage finished first, and then he leaned back in his chair, and gazed at me intently.

"Don't." I said, blushing.

"Don't what?"

"You know, look at me like that."

"It's kind of hard to not look at the person you're sharing a meal and conversation with." Gage smirked, then bit his lower lip. A breeze blew in and his robe opened, exposing a brown nipple on his hard chest. Now I couldn't stop staring.

"Yeah, but don't look at me like that."

"Like what?"

"All Casanova-like, smoldering." I pushed my plate away, his eyes following my every move.

"I'm smoldering? Like, you find me hot?" Gage snorted, trying not to laugh.

"Remember, we are trying to keep this thing we have between us as casual as possible. You looking all sexy and seductive is not helping." I tore my gaze away from him, and stared down at my lap, blood rushing to my cheeks.

"Babe, I can't help it. I am a Casanova. Looking all sexified comes naturally to me." Gage could barely contain his glee. One look at his face and I lost it.

We burst into laughter, and I realized all he had to do was stare at me precisely the way he was now, and I'd give him anything he wanted. Bastard.

"I've got tickets to an exhibition match at the PNC Arena for tomorrow night. Would you like to join me?"

"Um, well, what's an exhibition match? The word 'match' makes me think it's some kind of sportsball?" I'd never been a sports fan, but I remembered Gage playing on some sort of team when we were in high school.

"Yes, it's sportsball all right. It's played with a bright-yellow ball on a court with a net in the middle. Tennis. You used to watch me play back in high school." His face looked down, but his eyes remained on me, those thick dark lashes amping up the smoldering sex appeal. How could I say no to that? I nodded yes, and before I could speak, Gage's phone rang. He pulled it out of the pocket of his robe, and grimaced before shoving it back inside.

"Aren't you going to get that?" I asked, disturbed by his expression.

"No. It's my Dad. He never calls this late, unless he wants to yell at me about something." Gage abruptly stood and walked inside. Moments later, he returned with another open bottle of wine. He poured himself a glass, and then his phone rang again. Gage sighed, and pulled it out. He glared at it, then answered, "Dad, what's up?"

He looked away and stared toward the river, his prior sexy look replaced by frustration. Within seconds, I could hear his father's voice yelling on the phone. Gage's shoulders drooped, and he gulped his wine. When he spoke, his scowl was evident in his voice.

"No way, Dad. I'm not—"

Mr. Patterson cut him off with another tirade.

Overhearing them argue was making me uncomfortable. I started to leave the table to go inside, when Gage's hand snaked out and covered mine. He shook his head, and gestured for me to remain seated.

"Dad, it's nine o'clock," he said, glancing at his watch. "I have told you over and over again, I've tried everything to get that deal to go through. And, no, I will not meet with Donald Granger this late at night. Schedule it for first thing in the morning, but I'm off the clock now." Gage's voice shook, and from the sound of it, his father was ultra-pissed.

"Dad, I'm going now. If you want to stay up all night holding Donald's hand, go for it, but I am settled in for the night. The Granger deal can wait until the morning." Gage disconnected the call, then tossed his phone on the table, and buried his face in his hands. For a second I worried that he'd cracked the phone, but the rubber case protected it.

"Fuck me, my dad is a pain in the ass."

I was frozen, stuck to the chair, feeling embarrassed for Gage. From what I remembered, Frank Patterson had always been a hard ass. This wasn't the first time I'd heard him give his son hell. It was worse now than when we were teenagers, because of the man Gage had become. If this had been anyone else, I don't think Gage would have allowed them to speak like that to him. I had a suspicion his father was his Achilles heel.

"I'm twenty-eight years old, Lacey, and Dad treats me like I'm fucking twelve." Gage groaned through his fingers.

"He hasn't mellowed over the years, that's for sure." I murmured, then surprised myself by stretching a hand across the table. Gage eyed it through his fingers, then reached out and took it in his hand.

"I'd give anything to have a normal relationship with Dad, you know, him supporting me like parents are supposed to do. But, no matter what I do, it's never enough. I could sell ice to an Eskimo, an... and fuck him. Shit, I make us money, lots of it. I feel like his personal punching bag, and that's on a good day." He squeezed my hand and let go, then raked his fingers through his hair.

"Why do you keep working with him?" I asked, genuinely curious. I had no idea how he put up with it. My parents, while not perfect, were way more easygoing than Mr. Patterson.

"Because, deep down he's a good guy, been a good Dad when it counted the most. Whenever he dials up his inner asshole, I just think back on the times when he's saved my ass, and I manage to swallow my resentments and get back to work."

There was one slice of pizza left. "Are you going to eat that?" I gestured to the cardboard box on the table. Gage shook his head no. After I'd taken a couple of bites, he sighed and began speaking again, his voice different, the anger gone.

"What I wouldn't give to have a father like yours. I feel like nothing I do is good enough. I've spent my entire life trying to make the old man happy. At first, I tried to be as successful as he was. I thought building my own real-estate business and making a boatload of cash on my own would be a way to win his approval. Boy, was I wrong." Gage took a deep breath, started to say something else, then stopped.

"What is it?"

"I think he resents me. When I set up my business, he constantly ragged on it, telling me I could never be as good, or as successful as he was. That just drove me to work harder. Sometimes I just want to pull up stakes, move away, and start over somewhere else, so he'll leave me alone. Nothing I do is good enough, and I don't think he'll ever…" Gage stood up from the table and started pacing. "I'd give anything for him to just once give me credit for being good at what I do, for being a good son. My sister had the right idea. Dad wanted her to work for him too, but she said, 'hell no.' Opened her bar and kept a healthy relationship with Mom and Dad, well, with Dad anyway. She and Mom are like oil and water most days."

I could totally see that. Mrs. Patterson was like a modern day Carol Brady from the Brady Bunch, if I remembered right. She and her tattooed daughter must not have had much in common. I rose from the table and stopped Gage in his tracks.

"Kiss me."

He wrapped his arms around my waist, and his lips grazed my neck. Gage sighed and placed his head on my shoulder.

"Thank you, Lacey." Gage murmured in my ear.

"For what, Casanova?" I squeezed my arms around him tighter.

"For being here." He whispered, then he let go and strolled inside. Seconds later soft music filled the balcony. It was an old country song, and the woman's voice was a rich alto, her timbre melancholy as she sang about sweet dreams. Gage appeared at the entrance and started to speak, but hesitated. "May I have this dance?" He stammered, then tilted his head to the side. I walked over and draped my arms around his shoulders. Gage collapsed into me for a moment before straightening his spine. His feet started to move, and I followed along, his grip tightening around my waist.

"Who's this singer? Her voice is beautiful." I whispered, our bodies swaying together in the moonlight. I felt Gage's cock poking me through the thin fabric of his robe.

"Patsy Cline. Her voice soothes me, though your naked body wrapped around mine would go a long way toward—"

He crushed his lips against mine, and it was like the world stopped. My eyes shut, relishing the taste of him, his gently probing tongue exploring my lips, seeking a way in. My lips parted to let him go where he wanted to go. Soon my tongue was probing him too, and my arms wrapped around him tighter, holding him in place, so he would never go away. Damn, I wanted Gage, and not just in the bedroom. Maybe, if I could just accept the fact that this man would never hurt or abandon me, I had a chance of being truly happy.

Gage pulled back enough to nibble on my lower lip, then brushed his mouth across my cheek. I slumped into his arms, and without another word being spoken, he clutched my hand in his, and pulled me inside.

Chapter Seventeen

GAGE

I woke up before sunrise, hoping to get to the office before Dad and Mr. Granger. Lacey's head was on my chest, and I hated the thought of waking her up. I inhaled deeply, loving the smell of her. Hell, everything about Lacey, her skin, the thick blonde hair, her strong body combined with perfect curves. The entire package was everything I'd ever wanted. More importantly, there was the bond between us, the shared memories, and her unique ability to make me feel things no other woman on the planet could.

Her green eyes fluttered open for a second as I gently pulled myself out from under her, then she turned over and allowed me to rise from the bed. I tiptoed to my closet, turned on the light and sat at the dressing table in the middle of the room.

"Don't let them beat you down." I whispered to myself in the full-length mirror hanging on the wall. I'd barely slept last night, and the dark circles under my eyes were a dead give-away. It was strange, my thoughts while tossing and turning had alternated between dreading this upcoming meeting, and the elation of having Lacey in my bed. Then, I'd ruminated on the fact that Lacey wanted nothing more than a casual friends-who-fucked relationship, and wondered how long I'd manage to do that before losing my fucking mind.

"C'mon, get dressed. Why the hell have I still not put a coffee maker in here?" I mumbled, then lurched from my seat to figure out what to wear. I didn't normally dress up for work, usually a pair of casual slacks and a button-down shirt was my day-to-day uniform, but not today. I had to dress up a bit more, because of that asshole Granger, and decided on a black suit. Both of my ankles were in the trousers when the door flew open.

"I brought you some—" Lacey startled me. My ankles twisted in the pants and I fell forward, knocking the tray she was holding out of her hands. "Oh my god, Gage. I'm so sorry!"

I was flat on my back next to the tray she'd been holding. There was hot liquid under my head, the rich aroma of coffee filling the air. Lacey's hand flew to her mouth, her eyes wide open, frozen in shock.

"This day is turning out to be a doozy already." I muttered, then a giggle escaped. Seconds later I roared with laughter, rolling on the floor and clutching my stomach, while looking at Lacey's horrified face. "Babe, it's okay." I snorted out between guffaws.

Lacey continued staring down at me with her hand over her mouth, then I noticed her shoulders shaking.

"I can't help it." Lacey said, then started laughing too. She plopped herself on the chair and looked down at me, while I wiped tears from my eyes. Then, I glanced down and saw my slacks gathered at my ankles. I'd neglected to put on underwear, so everything was hanging out.

"Can you help me up?"

Lacey pulled me to my feet, then dropped to her knees to pull my slacks up as I swayed, appearing like I might fall again. I kinda exaggerated the swaying, enjoying her hands on my thighs as she held me in place.

"What about your suits, and the carpet? Gage, where is your cleaning stuff? The kitchen?" Lacey raced out of the room before I could answer. Maybe today wouldn't be as bad as I thought. Glancing in the mirror I noticed my expression. A goofy smile spread across my cheeks, and despite making a complete jackass of myself, I looked pretty fucking happy.

Lacey rushed back in and sprayed carpet cleaner on the rug to get the worst of the stains out. I'd already finished dressing, and got down on my knees to help her

"What about your clothes?" Her eyes circled the room. Except for the wall with the mirror, jeans, suits, slacks and shirts surrounded us. I kept it organized by color, and noticed the white shirts were spotted brown now. Lacey was biting her lower lip, not knowing whether to laugh or cry. I grabbed the rag out of her hand, threw it to the floor and laced her fingers through mine.

"It's okay. I'll call my maid Ruthie later, and get her to drop them off at the cleaners." I sighed, then felt my eyes filling with tears. I blinked them back, hoping Lacey didn't notice. "Lacey, thank you."

Her emerald eyes met mine, eyebrows raised. "Why are you thanking me? I ruined your—"

"Because I needed to laugh." I placed my hands on her shoulders and kissed her on the tip of her tiny, pert nose. I wasn't upset, and could honestly not care any less about the fucking clothes, or the stained carpeting. Her body relaxed into mine, and I reluctantly pulled away when I felt my dick responding. I still had that meeting to attend, damn it.

"Babe, this shit is replaceable, and the stains will come out. Seriously, they mean nothing to me. But you know what? The look on your face after I fell to the floor was priceless."

I drove around the block eight times before I could muster up the courage to park my truck. After the amazing night and crazy morning I'd had with Lacey, it was wrecking my stomach to even contemplate the tortures I knew were in store for me. I'd never been so nervous about a meeting before, and I hoped I had a few minutes to go over the contracts and maybe drink a cup of coffee, instead of wearing it.

"What the hell?" I muttered as I pulled into my parking space. It was seven in the morning, two hours before our doors officially opened, and Dad's car was already there. When I stepped out of the truck, I noticed a Lexus parked by the entrance. My caffeine-free gut twisted when I saw the license plate- DGRNGR.

Shit.

I was being ambushed, and didn't have time to prepare myself for the almost certain tongue lashing I would receive. Dad and Donald Granger had been friends for most of their lives, and both were hardcore as hell when it came to business. In fact, Mr. Granger was more bloodthirsty than Dad, if that was even possible. He'd stop at nothing to make an extra nickel, even if that meant chewing out my father, who in turn would make my life more miserable than he usually did.

I placed my hand on the front door and froze, afraid of

turning the brass knob. My eyes snapped shut, and I recalled the image of Lacey asleep, and then her laughing at my dumb ass on the floor of my closet. She'd agreed to go to the tennis match with me tonight, so at least I had something to look forward to. Plus, I'd fall over a million more times, just to see her face light up with glee, even at my own expense.

After hyperventilating for a minute, the acid in my stomach chilled out. I took a deep breath and pushed the door open. If I could have just five minutes to go over the files, I'd at least have a better chance of defending myself. Fuck, it didn't matter how much I'd offered that dude, what was his name again? Parker? I'd offered him far more money than he'd ever seen in his life, and he still wouldn't budge.

"Morning, Mr. Patterson." The security guard at the front desk mumbled, not looking me in the eye. Normally he grinned, even cracked a joke or two. Shit, Dad and Granger must have been bitching up a storm when they rolled up in here. I breezed past him and hit the button on the elevator.

When I turned on to the corridor where my office was located, I froze in my tracks; the door was open. Spinning on my heels, I leaned against the wall where they couldn't see me.

"What the hell am I going to tell them? Shit!" I whispered, wracking my brain, trying to figure a way out of this mess. Then, I remembered an old parking lot that was recently put on the market. It would cost far less than The Millbrook Arms, and since it didn't have a building on it, he'd save a bundle on demolition costs. And, it was on the same block as the apartment building.

"Yes!" I mouthed silently, and pumped my fist. That empty parking lot was the answer to my prayers, I hoped. Though I could barely recall the last time I'd been to mass, I crossed myself, then walked as confidently as I could into my office.

"About time you got here." Dad barked. He was seated behind my desk while Mr. Granger sat across from him. That left only one open seat next to the scowling old man.

"Good morning Mr. Granger. Dad." I started to sit, but at the last moment decided to lean against the wall, bumping against an award I'd won hanging there. If I needed to make a quick escape, I'd be closer to the door.

"Young man, you are disappointing me. That eyesore of a building should be emptied out by now. Have you even tried to get that loser out of there?" Mr. Granger's voice dripped with venom. I'd avoided eye contact with him and Dad so far, but now I had to look into his hooded eyes. Contempt was written all over his face, but his stare was especially hateful. Despite the air conditioning, trickles of sweat raced down my back.

"Sir, I've offered Mr. Parker much more than you originally budgeted. I've met with him multiple times and he refuses to sell."

"I'm prepared to make him a wealthy man. All he has to do is sign that building over to me. I don't think you've put forth your best effort. Let me be frank with you, kid. You're a spineless wimp who doesn't know how to get things done." Granger shook his head, his lips curled back over yellowing teeth.

"Gage," Dad squinted his eyes "I've been riding you hard over this deal, because Donald is one of our best clients." He raised an eyebrow at Mr. Granger and then surprised the hell out of me. "My son has worked his ass off, Donald. Gage has repeatedly—"

"Failed!" Mr. Granger snapped. "There's no good reason

why Parker hasn't signed that goddamned contract. All I'm hearing is one excuse after another."

"Sir, he's not selling, because he feels an obligation to the people who rent from him. Many of them would have no place else to go." I hoped he'd feel at least a little sympathy for the families that lived there.

"The scum who rent from him? A bunch of welfare queens and lowlifes, that's who they are. North Raleigh can support a much better class of people, people with money. That building is bringing down the value of every building in the area, including mine. And they will go whether you help me or not."

We glared at each other in silence for an uncomfortable moment. Why the hell was my father friends with this asshole? He was a heartless creep who didn't give a damn about anyone but himself. I shook my head with barely disguised disgust, and brought up the alternative property, which was a much better deal financially.

"Mr. Granger, recently an old parking lot on the same block as The Millbrook Arms was put on the market. The asking price is almost twenty percent less than what you initially offered Mr. Parker, plus you'd save a considerable amount on demolition costs." I crossed over to the desk and grabbed my laptop. "Let me show you the property."

"Don't bother." Granger's hand slapped my desk. "I want that eyesore gone. The Millbrook Arms should have been demolished years ago." The old man got to his feet. "Apparently, I will have to amp up the persuasion on Parker, since neither of you can get anything done."

Without another word he stalked out. Dad and I stared at each other with mouths opened.

"Shit." I muttered, shaking my head. I was going to get it now.

"I don't know what's gotten into Donald. Gage, I know you've done a lot of work to make this deal go through, but could you at least try one more time to get Parker to sell?" Dad walked around the desk and placed a hand on my shoulder, startling me. I was still trying to absorb the fact that he'd defended me for a change.

"Well?" The usual hard edge crept back into Dad's voice.

"Yes, sir. I'll get right on it." I muttered, though something felt off. A voice in the back of my head screamed that something wasn't quite right with what old-man Granger had said. My father knew the bastard better than I did. Maybe he'd know?

"Dad, wait a sec." I stopped him before he stepped out of my office. He turned in the doorway and crossed his arms over his chest. "What did Mr. Granger mean when he said he was going to amp up persuasion? He'd take a loss if he offered Parker any more money."

Dad's brow furrowed, and he sighed. "Son, you did the right thing offering him that parking lot down the street from the Millbrook property. Maybe it's a matter of pride?" He shut his eyes for a moment, then continued, "Gage, I know I give you a hard time, but it's because I want you to succeed. You've done everything you could do to make this deal go through." Dad shrugged his shoulders and walked out, and then he called back to me. "I don't have a clue what Donald meant."

"Fuck it." I muttered, then sat down to draft yet another contract for Parker to refuse.

Chapter Eighteen

LACEY

The PNC Arena was old, and about to be ripped down and replaced by a shiny new one. I remembered going to a concert here with Gage in our senior year. Back then it felt huge and modern, and I recalled feeling very grown up going to an actual concert filled with drugs, lights and screaming kids, without my parents dragging along behind me. Now it was seedy looking, the concrete floors cracked and dirty. For this tennis thingy they'd cleared out the stage in the center and erected a tennis court. Gage was in his element, blithely ignoring the surrounding decay, while his focus was entirely on the match.

"YES!"

Gage rose to his feet and roared as a tan lanky tennis player shot the ball into the net. I'd never seen this side of him before, and I hadn't a clue what was happening in front of us. The last time I'd been to a tennis match was in high school, and only because Gage was on the team. If I recalled correctly, Gage was the victor in all the matches I'd observed.

"Do you still play? I see courts all over the city." I leaned into him and whispered in his ear, visions of his muscled arms smashing balls on a tennis court filling my head. Then, it struck me how quiet tennis was in between points. On the few occasions I'd been to a baseball or football game, the crowd had been very noisy all the way through it. Tennis was almost dignified in comparison, except for the occasional curse screamed by one of the players. Kind of like Gage—regal, but with a coarse edge.

"Huh? Oh, nope, I can't. Shoulder injury in Afghanistan." Gage whispered back, his jaw clenched. Obviously a touchy subject. I'd never asked him about his time in the service, because I didn't want to stir up bad memories. Maybe I should find out what happened to him back then if I wanted to know who he was now? My feelings had grown, and while I had a general idea of his life over the last decade, I wanted to know more.

"How do you keep that studly body then?" I squeezed his bicep, then he bit his lower lip with those bright shiny teeth. My cheeks burned, wondering if I sounded stupid.

"I can't serve. If I swing my arm up, the way that guy is doing right now..." he pointed at the player tossing the ball in the air, "...over and over again, I'll be in agony for a solid week. I'm still able to lift weights and run, but with modified… yes!" Gage leapt to his feet again as one of the players did something very important, I guessed.

I stifled a laugh. His enthusiasm was endearing, and then I realized this was how he lived his life. Everything he did was in the moment, his glass always half-full and not half-empty as the old saying went. My former fiancé, Joseph, had been the opposite, always worried about appearances, the future, if the mail came on time. Hell, that was probably why he didn't show up on our wedding day. Hmm. Was I living my life in fear, instead of in the moment? Wondering if I could love someone and be loved in return? I glanced over at Gage, only to catch him staring at me. He placed his arm on the back of my seat and leaned in.

"What's going on? You look like you've seen a ghost." He murmured. I glanced down at the tennis court where the players were at the net shaking hands.

"I was trying to figure out what was happening down there, that's all." I leaned back into his arm, relishing the warmth against my shoulders. Gage wore a tight black t-shirt and blue jeans ripped at the knee, which was rubbing against mine. He was hot no matter what he wore, and today he reminded me of the boisterous boy I'd left behind.

"While you were figuring out the not-very-straightforward game of tennis, the taller guy won. The whole crowd got to their feet and cheered while you were deep in thought." He smirked, and I felt blood racing up my chest to my face. "You know, you're kinda sexy when you furrow your brows and stare off into the distance. Deep thinkers turn me on." Gage eyeballed the surrounding seats, and when he thought no one was looking he leaned in and pecked my cheek.

God, it would be so easy to fall in love with him. My heart thudded in my chest, a wave of happiness crashing through my head. I needed to say something, a diversion from what was happening between us, because... I didn't know. I couldn't think straight when Gage was breathing in my ear like that.

"If it's over, why is everyone still in their seats?"

"Because, there is one more match to be played." Gage peeked at his watch. "You hungry? We have about ten minutes before it starts."

"God, yes."

"Beer or soda?" Gage asked me. A teenager in a striped uniform drummed her fingers on the counter while waiting for our order.

"Diet whatever, and popcorn, extra butter."

"Diet soda to make up for the buttery popcorn?" He lifted an eyebrow, then told the kid what we wanted.

"You got it." I chuckled, then felt a tapping on my shoulder. I turned my head and was surprised to see Aunt Millie.

"What are you doing here, sweetheart? I didn't know you were a tennis fan." She grinned, and I noticed a rosy glow on her cheeks. She looked happier than I remembered, content.

"I didn't know you were one either." I opened my arms and gave her a hug. "Gage, do you remember my Aunt Millie?" I asked him when he handed me the popcorn and soda.

"Yes! Wow, it's been years. How have you been?" He placed his drink and popcorn on the counter and hugged her. She winked at me over his shoulder.

"Wonderful, especially now that Lacey is home again. Goodness, Gage, you look exactly the same as you did in high school. I'm so happy you and my niece are—"

"What is he doing here?" A gruff voice barked. I spun around and saw Bruce Parker strolling toward us. "Millie, this is that real-estate guy, the one who keeps badgering me to sell. Are you stalking me now too?" His eyes squinted toward Gage, his fists clenched. Gage's mouth dropped open, then he turned to the counter and grabbed our snacks. I could see his lips moving silently, then he spun slowly around.

"I'm not selling, no matter how many goons you send over to terrorize us." The older man bit off his words, then placed a protective arm around my aunt. Her eyes were like saucers, then they hardened.

"You're the man behind all of those so-called 'accidents'? A brand new boiler and a furnace breaking at once? The flooded basement? You are the crooked developer trying to kick those poor families out of their homes?" Her nostrils flared and then her focus shifted to me. Aunt Millie lifted an eyebrow and stammered. "Did... did you know about this Lacey? That he was the one behind those vicious attacks? You saw what those thugs did to that poor boy." Aunt Millie frowned, then her gaze turned icy. I understood her apprehension, but it irked me that she'd not even asked Gage for his side of the story. For that matter, how did Bruce come to his conclusions?

I thought about the building Gage and I lived in, and the undeniable wealth he'd amassed. Would he really hurt a group of poor people down on their luck, just so he could make a buck? I glared at him, then felt guilty for doubting him. I looked to the ceiling, then back at my aunt and Mr. Parker. Gage deserved the benefit of the doubt, but then I remembered that poor boy's arm, his swollen black eye.

"You're the real-estate developer that's trying to force—" I began.

"I don't know what you are talking about." Gage interrupted, "I know nothing about a little boy, or accidents, or thugs." He shrugged his shoulders, his face white as a sheet. His hands were trembling, and the top layer of his popcorn spilled to the concrete floor.

"Gage Patterson, you should be ashamed of yourself. Bruce is doing the community a service, providing affordable housing to families in the area. All you are interested in is money and making it off of the backs of those less fortunate than you." Aunt Millie was livid. "And you, Lacey Barnes, you might want to reconsider who you spend your time with." Her lips flattened into a straight line, and then she laced her arm around Bruce's and they stormed off. I turned to Gage, wondering if there was any truth to their accusations, but hating myself for even doubting his word.

"Babe, I swear, I know nothing about this. Yes, I met with Mr. Parker a few times, but I'd never, ever do anything like that." Gage pleaded. He glanced down at the spilled popcorn and mouthed the word 'fuck.'

My head was a wreck. What I needed was time to think, to process what my Aunt Millie and Mr. Parker were accusing him of. Our eyes locked, and it was almost like a game of chicken, both of us unwilling to look away. Finally, I shifted my gaze back toward the arena.

"Let's go back to our seats. Might as well enjoy the rest of the… tennis." I tilted my head toward the entrance to the arena, and we trudged back to our seats.

The last match had already started, and to be honest, it was just a blur of flying balls and cheering fans. Gage was subdued, his snacks abandoned on the floor by his feet. Unlike the first half of the evening, our shoulders were apart, knees planted solidly in front of us. A few minutes after we sat down, I felt the strange sensation of being watched. I scanned the crowd, only to find Aunt Millie's eyes glued to our seats. She and Mr. Parker were almost directly across from us on the other side of the tennis court. Her arms were crossed over her chest, and I felt the weight of her disapproval from fifty yards away.

I snuck a glance at Gage's profile, noticing his eyes on the floor instead of the match. He clutched the arms of the seat, and his shoulders were clenched. Misery was written all over his face, and I wondered if he'd noticed the death stare coming from my aunt. Damn it, as much as I wanted to believe him, I'd seen what those thugs had done to that boy, Tommy. His wreck of a mother struggling to keep it together for the sake of her child, and then unable to afford to buy him a little takeout Chinese. I knew this much; Gage had never lied to me before. Passing judgement before hearing both sides of a story wasn't something he'd do.

I leaned into Gage's shoulder, and whispered in his ear. "We need to talk."

I pushed myself up from the seat and scooted around him to the aisle, kicking his half-finished drink by mistake. "Shit." I muttered. Flustered, I jogged up the steps to the exit. When I got there, I turned and saw Gage picking up the empty drink cup and his bag of popcorn. He lumbered up the steps and tossed the garbage in the can next to the doors. I stepped into the corridor, turned and saw Gage hesitating. Anger flared in my chest.

"C'mon." I jerked my head in the opposite direction, and stomped off, then turned around to be sure Gage was following. He was shaking his head back and forth and mumbling to himself two steps behind me. Halfway down the hallway I leaned against the dirty gray wall, a jagged ball of anxiety spinning in my gut. The Gage I knew, or at least thought I knew would never do the things he'd just been accused of. But, I hadn't seen him in twenty years, didn't know the man he'd become in the interval. I thought about the wealth he'd accumulated, the stunning artwork hanging on the walls of his penthouse. Had he made his fortune at the expense of people struggling just to put a meal on the table? Or, was I still incapable of trusting him, or any other man for that matter?

"Gage, did you or did you not do the things Bruce Parker is accusing you of?"

He lifted his chin and fixed his eyes on mine.

"No. Lacey, this is the first I've heard of this. Yes, I've been to the Millbrook Arms, but only to make offers on the building for our client, that's it. I've done nothing beyond that. Hell, I don't even know how you'd go about finding people to do the things he's accused me of." Gage's eyes were wet. Whatever's happening to Mr. Parker and his tenants is wrong, and I'll do what I can to find out what's going on. But, I swear to you, I know absolutely nothing about it." He breathed. "Please, Lacey, you gotta believe me."

Either he was a very gifted actor, or he was telling me the truth. He stretched out his hand, palm open for me to grab if I wanted. I eyed it, wary, then realized there was no way he was behind the attacks. I trusted him, so I laced my fingers through his.

"I believe you."

Gage slumped against the wall beside me. "What happened? I know your Aunt Millie and Mr. Parker mentioned thugs and sabotage. What were they talking about?"

"For the last few weeks or months, they've had a bunch of accidents, and it all started when you started making him offers for the apartments." I put a finger on my chin, trying to figure out where Gage fitted in all this. "One of the children that lives there was brought into the ER after being beaten up. That's how I got involved. He caught a bunch of thugs trying to break into the building's basement if I recall it correctly. A twelve-year-old tried to stop them, and the bastards broke his arm."

"Shit." Gage ran his fingers through his hair. "No wonder Parker thinks I'm behind it. I swear I know nothing Lacey, I—"

"I trust you, Gage. I know you wouldn't... hey, your Dad —" I started, but Gage cut me off.

"My father is a miserable asshole on a good day, but that's not his style. He'd sooner cut his arm off than harm a kid." Gage paced in front of me. "Dad wants the deal to go through, but not like this. I'm there at the office every day, and I swear he conducts a clean business. We've always been on the up and up. Donald Granger, though, he's shady as fuck, or at least I think so."

"Who's that?"

"Granger is the man who wants to buy the building." Gage muttered, then he stopped pacing and grabbed my shoulders. "I'll talk to Dad tomorrow. We'll get to the bottom of this, I promise."

Chapter Nineteen

GAGE

"Damn it." I sputtered, placing the full cup of coffee back on my heated coffee thingy I'd bought to keep it warm, yet could never remember to turn on.

It was the third cup of coffee that had grown cold since I'd arrived at work. I had barely slept, and caffeine was a must if I was to get anything done today.

All I thought about as I tossed and turned in bed last night was Lacey, who'd opted to spend the night at her place, and what was happening at the Millbrook Arms apartments. It made me sick to my stomach, thinking about those poor people living there having their lives ruined by someone who didn't have a shred of humanity, only an eye for his bank balance. Plus, I couldn't bear the thought that Lacey might suspect me as being the man behind their misfortunes.

I gave up on sleep around five, and went to the gym downstairs, then headed into work early. Catching Dad before he got busy for the day was my top priority. We needed to talk, and it wasn't going to be pretty.

Deep in my heart, I knew my father had nothing to do

with the incidents plaguing Bruce Parker and his tenants. Dad would do anything to make a dollar, but harming innocent people was not his modus operandi. If it weren't for Donald Granger, we would have abandoned this deal weeks ago, but Granger refused to let it go. My gut was telling me Donald was behind the attacks, but until I had proof, there was nothing I could do about it.

I glanced at my phone, and saw that it was five after eight. Dad should be here by now, though I was surprised he hadn't popped his head in my door to yell at me already. Who knew? Maybe he was having his annual fifteen minute bout of happiness?

"Goddamn it, Cheryl, where the hell is Kristen? We were supposed to meet five minutes ago!" I heard Dad shouting in the hallway. I guessed the happiness theory was out the window, but I'd better catch him now before he got busy.

"Dad, please, just five minutes before your appointment. It's very important." I asked. He frowned and waved me into his office.

"Gage. I'm getting pissed off about the sales data from last month and—" Dad started, but I held my hand up to stop him.

"I'm not kidding, Dad, this is urgent." I perched on the edge of the wine colored leather couch in front of his desk. Our offices were totally different. His looked like the library at the country club, dark and oppressive. Dad rarely drew back the heavy damask curtains, and sat behind a huge oak desk. Mine was filled with contemporary furniture and artwork I'd brought from home, and the curtains were always open. I always felt like I was twelve years old and asking for an advance on my allowance when I was in his domain.

"Well, spit it out. I've got a full schedule today."

I took a deep breath. "Dad, someone is sabotaging the Millbrook Arms apartments, and it started when Mr. Granger became interested in the property."

"What the hell are you talking about, Gage?" Dad took his reading glasses off and lifted an eyebrow. "Sabotage? Exactly what do you mean by that?"

"I ran into Bruce Parker last night. He accused me of deliberately trying to force him out. They've had issues with their furnace, boiler, and electric box, plus—"

"That means nothing. Coincidences, that's all. It's an old property that's bound to have problems from time to time." Dad cut me off. He started to put his glasses back on, but he dropped them when I spoke the next sentence.

"A group of men beat up a kid, broke his arm." Dad's mouth dropped open. "The twelve-year-old boy caught them trying to break into the basement. These guys aren't messing around, Dad."

He stood, then circled the desk, and sat on the edge in front of me. He placed his index finger on his chin, then tried to speak, but I cut him off before he could begin.

"I think it's Mr. Granger, Dad. You and I run a clean business, so I hope you know I'm not accusing you of anything."

"Of course, Gage, I never thought you were." He plopped down on the couch next to me. "Donald and I go way back, graduated prep school together. He's an honorable man. I can't imagine he'd engage in these tactics. It must be someone else. Donald can't be behind this." His voice trembled. "Does Parker have any enemies?"

"Dad, he's a peace-loving, gray-haired hippie, a total throwback to the sixties. I seriously doubt he's pissed anyone off enough they'd attack little kids. This is someone trying to chase him and his tenants out, and I only know one man who fits the bill. Can you talk to Granger? Maybe he'd—"

"Son, it can't possibly..." He gave a deep sigh and rose from the couch." "I'll call him. Just to put your mind at rest. Mine too."

The morning dragged on, and I couldn't stop thinking about Bruce Parker. There had to be a clue, something that would tell me who was terrorizing him. My gut instinct said it was Donald. Dad had a ridiculous sense of honor when it came to his friends, unable to believe any of them could do something criminal. Several of his childhood buddies were successful businessmen, and a couple of them had gone to jail over their tactics. I saw Donald Granger in a different light. He was cold and calculating, and this wasn't the first time I'd felt uncomfortable around him. Out of all of Dad's friends, Granger had always been distant. At first I thought he simply hated me, but then I figured out he was like that with everyone.

"How the hell can I persuade Dad that his friend is—" Suddenly I remembered what he'd said in our meeting yesterday. That he was going to "amp up the persuasion on Parker."

"It's him, I know Granger's behind all this." I grabbed my phone and called Lacey. I couldn't imagine what else the bitter old man could do. Grabbing my jacket, I sprinted toward the elevator while waiting for Lacey to answer her phone. "C'mon, Lacey, pick up the damn phone."

"Gage. Why are you calling so early?" Lacey yawned. "It's my day off, I wanted to sleep in."

"It's Granger, I know it's Granger who's fucking with Parker." There was a group of people standing at the elevator, so I raced down the stairs instead. "Yesterday in our meeting, he said he was going to amp up the persuasion on Parker, do whatever it took to get him to sell. It's gotta be him. Lacey, I have a terrible feeling about this. I'm heading over to the Millbrook Arms to warn Mr. Parker." I threw open the door to the lobby and dashed outside to the parking lot.

"Oh my God, what if Aunt Millie is... I'll meet you there."

Black smoke filled the sky as I flew into the parking lot. Bright flames shot out of broken windows, and a crowd was gathered in the parking lot, many of them crying. One woman was being forcibly held back. Two men had her firmly in their grip.

"My son, let me go! I have to get my son!" A thin black woman wailed, fighting to make the men holding her back let go. Tears streamed down her face, her voice ragged from screaming.

"Where? Which apartment?" I yelled over my shoulder as I raced toward the entrance.

"Third floor, 3B! Please help my baby!"

By now I'd reached the door. I turned back and saw the woman collapse into the men's arms. When I reached for the doorknob it was too hot to touch. I yanked my jacket off and used it to open the door. Smoke poured out, and I couldn't see through my burning eyes. Then I heard a man yelling from upstairs.

"Tommy!"

By now, enough smoke had escaped and I could see the stairs. I took them two at a time, then noticed they were vibrating under my feet. The figure of a man was crouched on the second story landing. He was bent over coughing, and the door to the apartment next to him had amber and orange flames coming through it. It would only be a matter of seconds before the fire would burst through.

"Get out of there!" I screamed, then the man looked up. It was Parker. He tried to stand, but fell to his knees instead. Shit, I had to get the older man out. Pushing myself up the stairs was near impossible as wave after wave of intense heat pounded me back. When I reached him, I pulled him to his feet and flung an arm around his shoulder. He was gasping for air, wet trails of black and gray soot ran from his eyes.

"Let's go man, one foot in front of the other. I can't carry you." He nodded his head and coughed as I helped him down the stairs. Halfway down the building shook, and I felt the stairs shifting beneath our feet. Then the door of the apartment we'd been in front of upstairs blew off its hinges, sending flaming chunks of wood down the stairwell. Blinding fear took hold, and I tripped and fell down the last few steps, landing in front of the open door. Thankfully Parker landed next to me instead of on top.

"I got you!" A man's voice yelled, then I felt hands pulling me to my feet. In a flash, both Parker and I were stretched out on hot pavement. My lungs felt like they had spikes driven through them, and I struggled to breathe. Parker was curled up on his side coughing, and then the sound of that woman wailing propelled me to my feet.

"Tommy! Please help my boy. He's still in there!" She once again tried to break free from the men holding her back. Sirens screamed in the distance, but I knew they'd arrive too late.

"The fire escape." Parker wheezed. "His arm is broken, he can't make it down." He pointed at the side of the building. I looked up to the third floor and saw the frightened boy's face at a window. Two windows down from him vivid red flames were shooting out. He only had moments before the fire would take him.

I jumped up and pulled the rusty ladder down. The metal was scorching hot, but not bad enough I couldn't climb up.

"Please, save my baby!"

I heard the woman screaming over the wail of sirens. Each landing of the fire escape was an obstacle course of burning plants and melting plastic lawn chairs. I kicked the plants to the ground as I charged upward, not knowing if the boy would be strong enough to make it through the smaller fires.

When I got to the third floor, the boy was at the door waiting, his arm in a sling. There was no way he could have made the climb down without help. I scooped him up in my arms.

"Hold tight!" His legs gripped my torso while he tried his best to hold on to my neck. The boy's hold on me was tenuous, with his broken arm pushing against my chest. There was no way I could carry him down like that. Shit. God knows I didn't want to hurt him, but if it meant saving his life, I'd do what I had to do. I pulled his body tight against mine, and felt his arm crunch. His anguished scream rang in my ear, and then I felt him go limp.

"Sorry kid." I muttered, his hot face pressed against my cheek. Clutching him against my torso I descended the fire escape, and when I finally reached the last flight of steps, I felt a tug on the bottom of my pants. Bruce Parker was holding his arms out for the boy.

"He's out cold!" I yelled, and handed the kid over. Once Parker had a firm grip on him he ran toward the parking lot.

"Gage! Hurry!" Lacey's voice rang through the din. Smoke was swirling and I couldn't see where her voice was coming from. Then I felt a rush of heat and a roar in my ears, and the world went black.

Chapter Twenty

LACEY

"So it's definitely not Gage behind all of this." Aunt Millie said, breathing a sigh of relief. "I'm so sorry I doubted him, but Bruce has been going through so much hell. I'll apologize when we get there." I'd picked her up on the way to see Bruce, figuring she'd want to be there for him. I was ashamed to admit I'd had my own doubts.

"Well, unless he's warning Bruce about himself, then... is that what I think it is?" Plumes of black smoke spiraled into the air from a distance. The windows were open and an acrid smell filled my nostrils.

"I've got an awful feeling about this, Lacey." Aunt Millie's voice dropped to a whisper. She dug through her handbag until she found her phone. "I'm calling Bruce."

My foot stepped harder on the gas as I raced through a yellow light. I glanced over at my Aunt whose forehead was wrinkled in worry. The hand not gripping her phone was squeezing my thigh.

"Damn it, he's not answering."

"We're almost there. Let's just hope…" The words died in my mouth. It was definitely the Millbrook Arms. From two blocks away we could see it, orange and violet flames shooting from the roof.

Oh my God, Gage.

What if he was hurt? Images of him trapped in a burning room careened through my mind. I shook my head. Flaking wasn't good, and it would be too easy to fall prey to it with Gage in my head. They might need my help.

"I'm parking a block away to leave room for the firemen." I pulled into an abandoned gas station. Aunt Millie flung the car door open, and was halfway up the block before my feet hit the pavement.

A woman was being held back by two men, wailing and cussing that they let her go. Halfway up the block, my heart nearly stopped. It was Latrice Jenkins, and I knew there was only one reason she'd be freaking out.

"Lemme go, you son of a bitch!" She elbowed one of the men in his stomach, and to his credit, he only tightened his grip on her arms. When she saw me her bloodshot swollen eyes widened. She stopped struggling for a moment, and then she screamed, her voice chilling my bones.

"Tommy! Please, oh help me, Jesus, help my boy. He's still in there!"

Frozen in place, years of training in how to deal with real-life emergencies were forgotten. I was paralyzed, frantically praying Gage was okay, that he hadn't gotten here yet. I knew he'd be the first one in the building, putting his life at risk to save everyone.

I shook my head, clearing it as best I could. Latrice and Tommy didn't deserve this, the other residents who stood there in shock as their homes burned to the ground hadn't done a single thing to warrant this destruction. I scanned the parking lot, hoping to see Gage pulling up in his truck, but then I saw it parked on the far side of the lot.

My heart sank.

I had to focus, damn it. People were sitting on the curb coughing and gasping for air, so I ran in their direction to see who the medics should treat first, hoping Gage was nearby, and safe.

Most of them were suffering from smoke inhalation, and after a cursory glance I knew they'd be okay. A few elderly women needed oxygen, and I'd not seen anything more than a couple of first-degree burns. Thank God their smoke alarms alerted them in time. Then I saw Bruce limping in my direction. His arms were beet red, and his long gray hair was flattened against the sides of his face. I didn't have a first aid kit, but the sound of sirens in the distance eased my mind. Bruce looked like he'd been through a war. His body shook as I examined him, and he kept glancing over his shoulder.

"Bruce, your arms are burned, but I can't tell how bad it is. There should be an ambulance here any second." I reassured him, and also tried to reassure myself, but then he destroyed my composure.

"Your friend, Gage," he coughed, then fell to his knees on the pavement. "He's up there!" Bruce pointed toward the side of the building. The smoke obscured my view, so I stepped forward, and the intense heat made my hands fly up to my face. Finally, I glimpsed Gage. He was carrying someone down the metal steps. It had to be Tommy. The boy was limp in his arms. An intense bolt of fire burst through the window next to him, breaking the glass.

"Oh God, this can't be happening." I moaned, then felt someone run past me; it was Bruce. He stood underneath the fire escape holding out his burnt arms for the boy. Another flare of bright orange shot out the broken window just a few feet from where Gage was lowering Tommy into Bruce's arms. Once Parker had a firm grip on him, he rushed to the parking lot where the first fire truck had just pulled in. Instinctively my feet began to move, running as close to the fire escape as I could before the heat shoved me back.

"Gage! Hurry!" I yelled out. He was about to drop to the ground from the ladder when a huge boom and blinding light knocked me over. The smell of sulfur filled the air as I frantically got to my feet and searched through the clouds of smoke billowing across the parking lot.

"Where is he? Oh my God, where is he?" I yelled, then felt a tug on my arm. Aunt Millie was coughing and pointing to the left. "I saw him flying through the air."

Gage was face down on the ground beside the chain-link fence surrounding the building. I raced to his side and gingerly turned him over, and what I saw ripped my heart to shreds. He was unconscious, but he was gasping for air. Placing my hands on his chest I examined his ribcage. He'd broken some ribs in the fall, and possibly punctured a lung. I bit my lip, trying to hold back the tears. There was no way I could help him if I couldn't control myself. "Damn it, Gage, you can't—"

"We've got this, ma'am, please back away." A rough voice barked in my ear.

I swiveled my head at the sound of the paramedic's voice, then a gurney dropped beside us.

"I'm a nurse. He's broken some ribs, but I also think he's punctured a lung. I'm riding with him in the back of the ambulance."

"They're taking him into surgery now." Powell said, then handed me a cup of coffee. "I'm so sorry, Lacey." I nodded my thanks and then he patted me on the shoulder and walked away. I'd never been in this position before, in a hospital waiting room, anxiously waiting to know what was going on with someone I cared about. Never again would I not have anything except the utmost sympathy for those agonizing over the pain of a loved one.

Loved one? Did I really just admit to myself that I loved him? Sometimes it took the shock of potentially losing the one you cared about the most to realize that, yes, they were the most important person in your life. But I still wondered... it just seemed like everything had happened so damn fast. Should I trust my emotions right after experiencing such intense trauma with him?

The heavy sound of boots approaching caused me to look up. Gage's sister Inky was racing toward me from the emergency room entrance.

"How is he? Please, tell me he's going to be okay." She sank down into the seat next to me, placing her hand on mine. She was in sweats, and her hair was a tangled black mess. Without her usual goth makeup on, she looked acutely vulnerable. I didn't know how to reach Gage's parents, then remembered we'd exchanged numbers. I'd called her as soon as we arrived at the hospital while she'd still been asleep.

"He's in surgery. Gage has two broken ribs, and a punctured lung. He also has a concussion, plus second-degree burns on his arms and neck." My voice rasped, still scratchy from the smoke. Inky swallowed back a sob.

"What the hell was he thinking playing the hero? He could've been—" She started, but a tremendous sense of pride filled my chest. I held my hand up and interrupted.

"You would have been so proud of him. Gage rescued a boy, a child with a broken arm trapped in his apartment. If it wasn't for him, that kid would be dead." I squeezed her hand, and she sank back in the hard plastic seat.

"I'm... fuck, I'm sorry. It's just he's so fucking impulsive sometimes. He's the type who stops bar fights, the one who protected me from bullies when we were kids. It feels great when he does this shit, but sometimes I wish he'd back off, stop putting himself in danger. I know, I'm selfish, but I don't want anything to happen to him." She placed her face in her hands and let out a soft wail. When she looked up again wet trails of tears snaked down her cheeks. I rubbed her back, then wiped my eyes with the back of my other hand.

"I'm going to kill that asshole, and don't you dare try to stop me, Mary." Frank Patterson's deep voice carried through the waiting room as the sliding doors opened. Mrs. Patterson saw us and took her husband's hand. Unlike her daughter, she was dressed impeccably in a pink and blue dress, but with streaks of black running down her cheeks.

"How is he? What happened?" She sat on the other side of Inky, while Mr. Patterson made a beeline for the nurses' station. Poor Powell was about to get an earful.

Inky turned to me, so I filled her mother in on the events of the morning. When I was done, she pulled a tissue out of her purse and handed it to Inky, then pulled a compact out and started to clean her face. A few moments later her jaw dropped and her head swung in my direction.

"Lacey? Lacey Barnes? When did you get back in town?"

"About a month ago."

"Well, that explains everything." She actually smiled, then dabbed at her eyes again with the tissue.

"Excuse me?" I enquired, wondering what on earth she was talking about.

"Gage has been so moody lately. He was even short with me a few times, and he's never been like that before."

"I don't understand. What does that have to do with me?"

"Lacey Barnes, I wasn't born yesterday. He was in love with you when you were in high school together, and I don't think he ever got over you. Now that you're back, he's a mess." She reached across Inky and patted me on the knee. "I'm grateful you were there for him in his time of need this morning."

Inky nodded her head and shrugged. "Yeah, Lacey, Gage's got it bad for you."

Jesus Christ, had I been so blind? I knew he wanted us to become more serious, but I had no idea about the depth of his feelings. Had I been pushing him away too much?

"They don't have any news yet. I swear to god I'm going to kill that son of a bitch." Mr. Patterson was back from harassing the nurses, and was pacing in front of us. Inky got to her feet and hugged him.

"Dad, calm down or you're going to have a heart attack or a stroke, or something really, really bad." He kissed her cheek, then glanced in my direction. "Why aren't you up there?" He jerked a thumb toward the nurses' station.

"Frank, don't you remember who she is? Lacey Barnes. She was Gage's girlfriend back in high school. She rescued

Gage today. You owe her a great deal of thanks." Mrs. Patterson said, then she glanced up to the ceiling and shuddered. "Thank God you were there for him."

"Oh. I thought you looked familiar. You're the reason he's been acting so funky lately." He patted me on the shoulder, then he shook his head, and grimaced. "Donald fucking Granger is going to—"

"Frank, watch your language." Mrs. Patterson clucked. Inky giggled, and I sank deeper into my seat. "Trish, stop laughing. It only encourages your father." Inky guffawed and then started sobbing again. Her mother rubbed her back, while Mr. Patterson stalked over to the nurses' station to yell some more.

Some things never changed. After all these years, Gage's family was still fucking nuts.

"The surgery went as well as could be expected. Gage is going to be just fine. It will be another hour or so before you can see him. He'll probably still be feeling the effects of the anesthesia, so he might not be very with it." Powell delivered the good news. "I'll let you know when you can visit with him as soon as possible."

By this time the waiting room had filled up with residents of the Millbrook Arms. As composed as Mrs. Patterson usually was, she lost it completely when Latrice Jenkins shyly approached. I told the woman she was Gage's mother, and her eyes flooded with gratitude.

"Your son saved my son's life."

The two women held onto each other, both weeping for their boys. By this time I knew I couldn't stay any longer. I had too much to think about, feelings to examine, and decisions to make. Now that I knew Gage would recover, I strolled over to the elevator. I didn't want to spark conversation by walking out of the main entrance, so I went up to the next floor, and left through the employee exit.

Chapter Twenty-One

GAGE

"You didn't happen to see Lacey at the nurses' station?"

Inky dropped my hand and laid hers on my forehead. She bit her lower lip, and I already knew the answer before she could say it.

"No, but remember she works in the ER, so she might be, you know, busy or something." She glanced out the window, then sat in the chair next to the hospital bed.

"Maybe I should rephrase that. Have you seen her at all today?" I asked, my voice flat. She shook her head.

"Gage, I have no idea what's going on inside her head. Lacey slipped out last night, and I haven't seen her since. I almost knocked on her door before I came today, but I felt that might be overstepping a boundary or something."

"When has that ever stopped you before?" I muttered, feeling numb inside. Lacey hadn't shown up. By noon I figured she wouldn't. I knew why she wasn't here, but I wasn't ready to face that just yet, not with my sister staring at me with that pitiful look in her eyes.

"You never know what could happen, Gage. She could

walk through that door any—" She started, but I couldn't bear to hear any more platitudes.

"Enough matchmaking optimism, okay? Would you mind it terribly if I could be alone for a while?" The last twenty-four hours had drained me, physically and emotionally. I needed space. Inky kissed my forehead.

"You got it. Call me if you need anything, or let Ruthie know. She can drop off anything you want from home at my place, and I'll bring it to you." She squeezed my hand, then left.

I glanced at the bandages on my arms, then the IV drip at my side. It was worth every bit of pain to save that little boy, but I seriously wished I could lose all the machines and bandages. The only thing I regretted was not being able to see Lacey, and I had a sinking feeling I wouldn't be laying eyes on her anytime soon.

"Lacey, what the hell did I do?" I whispered to myself. Of course, I knew the answer to that question. I'd pushed too hard, tried to rekindle what was, in her mind, a teenage romance. Lacey was a different person now, and no matter how hard I tried to bring us back together, she just wasn't interested.

I knew that I couldn't keep things casual any longer with her. I wanted it all, her mind, body and soul. It would be difficult to give up the passionate sex we had shared, but if she couldn't provide all three, then I'd have to go back to my old ways. Problem was, the thought of fucking around with a stream of anonymous women, now left me cold.

"Ha!" I laughed, then regretted it. "Shit." I wrapped my free arm without the IV over my chest. It hurt to laugh, but it was funny to think that I, Gage Patterson, was no longer interested in random encounters. In fact, this was the very reason I'd never gotten involved with anyone since Lacey left ten years ago. I watched my friends put themselves through one agonizing relationship after another, and for what? Sex? Fuck that, I could scratch that itch anytime I wanted to, without the insane baggage of being tied to a single woman.

Tears raced down my cheeks again. All day long, even through visits from Mom and Dad, I'd been tearing up, just barely able to keep from blubbering like a baby. Mom went so far as to ask a nurse if that was a side effect of the pain meds. Thank God she said it was, but I knew better.

All I wanted was one specific girl now, and Lacey wanted nothing to do with me.

"Would you mind turning the TV off for me?" I asked the nurse as she prepared to leave. One of my visitors had switched it on and dropped the remote out of my reach. It was showing an old movie, one of my favorites in fact, An Affair to Remember starring Cary Grant. It was the story of a couple who fell in love, but both were involved with other people. They'd agreed to meet in six months time to see if they could pick up where they had left off. Now I couldn't bear to watch it. She was very motherly, so she plumped up my pillows, patted my hand, then turned off the television and left.

All I could think about was Lacey, and the reality of what we had between us. Friends with benefits, and that was all she wanted. Hell, I wasn't sure if she even wanted that anymore. Whenever I was alone today I spoke aloud, high on the drugs, and not caring how crazy all this talking to myself must be.

"You know, Lacey, I'd do anything for you. Why the hell

won't you let me in? This is insane. Why don't you want me the way I want you? Nothing beats—" The door slowly opened, and I had the good sense to shut up.

"Knock knock." Lacey stuck her head in the door. "Want some company?"

My throat thickened and I couldn't answer, so I nodded my head instead. I wondered if she was here to let me down gently, you know, the polite way of dumping someone. Or maybe this was a hallucination brought on by the painkillers? Nah, Lacey was nothing but a polite, kind woman, who had enough respect for me to let me down in person. I sighed and waited for the dumping to commence.

Lacey perched on the edge of the bed, and that was when I noticed her chin trembling. I glanced down at her hands which were shaking too. Well, at least she felt guilty about dumping my ass. Lacey's brilliant green eyes were damp, threatening to spill over. Fuck, I'd had enough tears to last a lifetime, and if she started weeping, so would I.

"I've never been so terrified in my life, Gage Patterson. The thought of losing you made my blood run cold." Lacey breathed, then she took my hand in hers. "I apologize for not coming sooner, but I had a lot of thinking to do."

I nodded, the lump in my throat growing bigger.

Lacey turned away and glanced out the window, but her fingers locked more firmly into mine. I felt a tear sliding out of the corner of my eye. Lacey had my one good hand, so I couldn't brush it away, so I shut my eyes instead.

"I love you, Gage Patterson. I was crazy not to own it, scared of being hurt again. But, you are the only man in my entire life who makes me feel the things that I do. I don't want to continue on the way we have been. There's nothing casual about the way I feel, and the only way I want you is if

I can have you all to myself. Will you forgive me for being such an ass?"

My eyes popped open, and more tears fell. Lacey's lips parted and then shut, then she bent over and placed her mouth on mine. My lips trembled, unable to open, until I felt her tongue gently pushing against them.

This had to be a dream, because she tasted even better than I remembered. Her arms wrapped around me as best she could, and I felt my chest expanding, filling up with something I couldn't name. Lacey Barnes had just said she loved me, and she was kissing me now, and I couldn't imagine anything in the universe finer than this.

Then, the door flew open. "Mr. Patterson, are you okay? Your heart-rate monitor is going nuts." She was right, and neither of us had noticed the insane beeping from the stupid machine next to the bed. The nurse glanced at Lacey, who was still in her scrubs. "Of all people, you should know better than to get a patient excited like that. I need you two to calm things down." She shook her finger at us, winked, then quietly shut the door behind her.

"Hey, I know it's kinda crowded, what with all these doohickies sticking out everywhere, but could you lie down beside me?"

Lacey spread out on the side without the IV, taking care not to hurt me. Once she was settled in, I said the words I'd been dying to say since she'd walked back into my life.

"I love you, Lacey Barnes, I always have and I always will."

Epilogue

LACEY- SIX MONTHS LATER

It was 90s music night at Inky's bar. Powell, who said he had exciting news, invited Gage and me, though Inky and I had a surprise of our own. Ever since Gage was hospitalized, Powell and Inky had become super chummy, so I had a feeling she already knew what his news was about.

We sat in the back at Gage's usual table surrounded by friends. Cameron and Marcy were there, and oddly enough, Zack, the part-time bartender was there too. Normally he kept to himself, but he was a cool guy, so it pleased me to see him relaxing with the rest of us.

"So, Gage, what's the status on the Granger guy? I've followed along in the newspaper, but I'm sure you know more than they do." Marcy asked, then took Cameron's hand in hers.

"He's going down, hard. Even if he escapes a prison term, which is doubtful, he's facing multiple lawsuits. Dad is suing him for defamation of character, and breach of contract. Bruce Parker and the residents of the Millbrook Arms have also filed a civil suit. I'm considering one of my own, though I dare say after Dad's through with him, he won't have a pot to piss in." Gage grinned, then slid his arm over my shoulders.

"So, what's happened to the people who lived there? I read that you are helping them out." Cameron asked.

"I bought an older building on New Bern Avenue, and with some grants from the city, it's being refurbished, and then I'm gifting it to Bruce Parker. He's also getting a decent settlement from the insurance company, so he can expand the apartment building if he wants. The building next door has another twenty units, and it's been vacant for years. In a way, this tragedy has worked in his favor. He'll be able to help more people down on their luck with affordable housing than he ever could have before." Gage turned to me. "I heard your Aunt Millie is shacking up with him now."

"Yes. Bruce moved into her house about a week ago. She's never been happier."

"Hey, guys. Scoot over, Lacey." Gage and I moved, so Powell could sit next to us. Inky pulled a chair from another table and sat at the end. Powell was practically bouncing in his seat, and I knew whatever he had to tell us would be big.

"So what gives?" I elbowed him. "Are you going to tell us your big news, or do we have to force it out of you?" Powell blushed, then he glanced at Inky, who nodded her head.

"Okay. This isn't just one announcement, it's several, but they're all tied together." He sipped his beer, then threw back a shot of whatever Inky had set in front of him. Powell wiggled his eyebrows, and then he dropped the bomb.

"I gave my notice to the hospital today."

"You what?!" I spat out. How the hell would I get through those long shifts without my favorite buddy?

"I don't talk about this much, but I only went into nursing, because what I really wanted to do was unlikely to make me a decent living. Now that has changed." Powell took a deep breath, then his words tumbled out of his mouth in a torrent. "I've been a cellist since I was a kid, and in fact I have two degrees, the first from Berklee College of Music. Jobs with orchestras are ultra-competitive, and after auditioning around the country on every weekend and vacation I've had in years, I finally got a job offer. Guys, you don't know how long I have waited for this to happen!"

"Congratulations!" Gage smiled, then lifted his glass. "To Powell, who never gave up on his dreams!" Everyone lifted their glasses, and then a horrible thought struck me.

"Wait a second. You said you've been auditioning all over the country. Does this mean you're moving?" Damn, we'd grown close over the last few months, and I hated the thought of him moving away.

"Well, I am moving, but it's not as far as you think." Powell lifted his mug and smirked, before taking a drink. "I got a job with the Raleigh Symphony Orchestra. Inky, you tell them the next part."

She clapped her hand on his shoulders and grinned. "Well, you guys know I've been trying to rent out the space next door for a couple of years now. Powell is not only becoming a famous musician, the two of us are opening a coffee shop and bookstore next door, and he will live upstairs from it!"

"Oh, thank God! That's so awesome!" I breathed a sigh of relief. Having Gage back in my life was the best gift the universe had ever given me, but my friendship with Powell meant a lot too. Despite Raleigh being my hometown, I didn't know that many people yet. Powell and everyone else at this table had come to mean a lot to me over the past few months.

"Oh, and before we finish all these congratulations, there is one more announcement." Powell gestured across the table toward Zack. "Meet the new manager of Jacked Up Coffee And Books, Zack Bronstein."

Zack blushed and grinned from ear to ear. It looked like lots of changes were in store for our group of friends. I glanced over at Gage, then at Inky. She mouthed, "Are you ready?" I subtly nodded, and she got up from the table and raced over to the DJ. A minute later the song changed, and it just so happened to be the song Gage and I had come to call our own. We'd spent many nights on his balcony swaying in each other's arms to Truly Madly Deeply by Savage Garden. I looked over at him and a small smile danced across his face.

"May I have this dance?" I whispered in his ear.

"I would never pass up a chance to hold you in my arms. After you."

Powell stood to let us pass, then I took Gage's hand and led him to the makeshift dance floor, which we had all to ourselves. He wrapped his arms around my waist and pulled me in tight. As always, I inhaled deeply, relishing his clean woodsy scent.

"Every time we dance to this song, I think about how close we were to losing each other. I never want to spend a day without you by my side, Gage Patterson." I breathed in his ear. He pulled me in closer, placing a hand on that in-between place that wasn't quite my back, and also wasn't my ass. I loved it when he touched me there.

"I feel something hard on my leg. Not that I'm complaining…" I teased, then I nibbled on his earlobe and he fell into me for just a quick moment. I snuck a glance over to our table. Inky was rolling her hands in a circle with a look on her face telling me to hurry. I never thought this day would come, and suddenly I was petrified. What if... damn it, just do it already.

"Gage?"

"Yes?"

I reached behind me and removed his hands from my back. His eyes squinted, and he started to say something, but stopped. I dropped to my knees in front of him, and he looked even more perplexed. The DJ cut the music off and the bar grew silent.

"Gage Patterson, you are the most stubborn and lovable man I've ever known. When I first met you, I was so empty inside, afraid of feeling anything, numb in fact. You've changed that for me. Now I have something beating in my chest again. You're rewritten my heart, and I want to let the future in, but only if you're in it. I can't imagine living another day without you, and I feel like we were robbed of too many years already." The room grew blurry for a moment, and I forced myself to keep speaking. "Will you marry me? I know it's usually the man who asks, but I'm too impatient to wait for you, because I can't imagine anything else I want more than having you with me every day for the rest of my life." My heart was galloping a mile a minute. When I looked up, tears were streaming down Gage's cheeks, then he reached for my hand and pulled me to my feet. He reached into his pocket and pulled out a small, velvet box.

"Damn it, of course I'll marry you, Lacey. Um, it's kind of funny, but I bought this yesterday, and I was waiting for the right time to give it to you." He swiped at his eyes. "I guess this is as good a time as any." Gage opened the box and took my hand in his, then slid the most stunning ring on my finger. An emerald, with a pearl on each side of it.

Now it was my turn to blubber. I could barely see anything through my tears, and I wondered at the beauty of this man, the one I'd done my best to keep at arm's length.

Gage's lips crashed against mine, and the usual high I got from his kiss was magnified by a thousand. My legs shook, and I was afraid I'd fall to the floor. Then I broke the kiss, and we faced the bar where every patron was cheering us on. Gage's eyes grew wide and he glanced around the room, almost as if he'd forgotten anyone else was there.

A huge smile spread across his face, then he gave an embarrassed little wave, and whispered in my ear, "I love you, Lacey."

The End

About the Author

Ella Sage is from the American south and loves nothing more than to curl up with a delicious romance novel and a cup of tea. This is her first novel.

www.ingramcontent.com/pod-product-compliance
Ingram Content Group UK Ltd.
Pitfield, Milton Keynes, MK11 3LW, UK
UKHW041827200726
13854UKWH00002BA/614